THE VOICES OF THE CHILDREN

PARTHIAN

LIBRARY OF WALES

George Ewart Evans was born in 1909, in the mining village of Abercynon. He was one of a family of eleven children whose parents ran a grocer's shop – the setting of his semi-autobiographical novel *The Voices of the Children* (1947). After education at Mountain Ash County School and University College Cardiff – where he read classics and trained as a teacher – he had ambitions of being a writer. He published verse and short stories – many with a Welsh background – in various literary journals, and extracts from *The Voices of the Children* first appeared in *The Welsh Review* in 1945.

In 1934 he became a teacher in Cambridgeshire, where he met his wife, Ellen. After his wartime RAF service, they settled permanently in East Anglia and raised four children. In 1948 he gave up teaching and turned from writing fiction to producing a sheaf of studies, now regarded as classics, based on conversations with his elderly East Anglian neighbours – farm workers and rural craftsmen – from whom he acquired a wealth of knowledge about their vanishing customs, work habits, and superstitions. His *Ask the Fellows Who Cut the Hay* (1956) marked him out as an original and sensitive interpreter of English rural life, and books like *The Pattern under the Plough* (1966), *Where Beards Wag All* (1970), *The Days That We Have Seen* (1975), and *From Mouths of Men* (1976, in which he returned to the South Wales coalfield), established his reputation as a pioneer in the field of oral history.

He died in Brooke, on the Norfolk/Suffolk border, in 1988.

THE VOICES OF
THE CHILDREN

GEORGE EWART EVANS

LIBRARY OF WALES

Parthian
The Old Surgery
Napier Street
Cardigan
SA43 1ED
www.parthianbooks.co.uk

The Library of Wales is a Welsh Assembly Government initiative
which highlights and celebrates Wales' literary heritage in the
English language

The publisher acknowledges the financial support of the Welsh
Books Council

The Library of Wales publishing project is based at
Trinity College, Carmarthen, SA31 3EP
www.libraryofwales.org

Series Editor: Dai Smith

First published in 1947
© The Estate of George Ewart Evans
Library of Wales edition published 2008
Foreword © George Brinley Evans 2008
All Rights Reserved

ISBN 978-1-905762-514

Cover design by Lucy Llewellyn
Cover image: The Hopkins Children (photographer unknown)
Printed and bound by Dinefwr Press, Llandybïe, Wales
Typeset by books@lloydrobson.com

British Library Cataloguing in Publication Data

A cataloguing record for this book is available from the British
Library.

LIBRARY OF WALES

FOREWORD

I first met the writer of *The Voices of the Children* through Doctor Thomas, our local GP, to whom George Ewart Evans dedicated his oral history of mining life, *From Mouths of Men*. It happened in a round about way. I was stuck in the house recovering from an accident at work; I was watching too much television and complaining too much about it to Peggy, my wife. She suggested, not so politely, that if I thought I could do better I should write something myself. So I did. A friend typed it and we sent it to the BBC and, lo and behold, I was invited up to London to 'discuss your script'. Doctor Thomas was delighted – he always believed in keeping his patients active – but because I was still under his care he was also concerned. It was March 1963, the whole country was frozen solid and I was still in a pretty fragile state. I had lost an eye in the accident. But I went anyway.

The man I had to see at the BBC was Harry Green, a well known television script writer, from Neath. He met me at the reception.

'George?'

'Mr Green?'

'Harry will do, George. Tell me, George, is it still bloody blowing in Banwen?' As a young reporter in the early 1930s he had been sent to report on an explosion at Onllwyn No.1 colliery, near Banwen. 'I got off the bus by the Onllwyn Inn and the wind almost cut me in half.'

Over a cup of tea in the canteen he set out my options. 'Your work is good, George. That's why I wanted to speak to you. Take it home and put it between two cardboard covers. Don't be disappointed. In this place they eat seed potatoes.'

It was 1963, still black and white TV, and I had written a drama taking place in the darkness of a coalmine. But Dr Thomas insisted I get a second opinion. I sent it to Kitty Black, who was the head of drama at Rediffusion. I was invited to London again. They offered me a job. 'Come and work at the studios. See how they do it. Then you'd get to know exactly what a TV camera could and couldn't do.' There was no mention of any money.

I returned home on the train. I had a wife and two young boys who were both in school. I needed to earn a living. When I got back to Banwen I burnt the script on a bonfire in the back garden.

A good ten years on and Dr Thomas had become a

regular visitor to the house. He liked Peggy's Welsh cakes and the warmth of my kitchen. I'd gone back to industry but not mining. A friend of his was researching a book and he asked would I, as an ex-miner and would-be writer, be willing to be interviewed. He was writing a book about men who had worked in the anthracite coalfield.

Two days later, George Ewart Evans was in my kitchen. He was distinguished looking, quietly spoken and charming: the published writer had arrived. Dr Thomas had told him about my own writing and my ambitions for it.

That summer George Ewart Evans became engrossed in life back in a coal-mining community, like the one of his own youth. He relished being in the company and being able to talk at length to men like Jeff Camnant, who was responsible for driving the main cut into the Cornish drift. Jeff was a bear of man who voraciously read books that arrived through the post. Or Huw Hughes (so short on the day he started work, his Davy lamp bumped along the ground). Or John Williams, Cwmtwrch, who started work as a collier boy in 1918 and who, by the time he was being interviewed by Ewart, was one of the country's most competent and respected mining engineers.

These men embodied the very characteristic George Ewart Evans cherished most: integrity. A quality that seemed to come naturally to men who, during their working day, risked their lives to earn a crust.

Over that summer we became good friends. He wrote me a letter in September 1973, asking me to make sketches illustrating and explaining the opening out of the Rhas drift – how they drove the drift, made double-partings, then the branching out to make levels, and the companion drift, and the two levels, and then the headings. On these sketches the illustrations by Peter Branfield in *From Mouths of Men* are based.

And in the same letter he wrote, 'I very much enjoyed listening to your account, and admire your turn of phrase. After listening to the tape and making a transcript, I am sure you should return to your writing even if it gives you less time for your painting. You have a feeling for words and it would be a pity to neglect this entirely.'

I did as he advised and he was instrumental in getting my first short story, *Boys of Gold*, published in *The Anglo-Welsh Review*, in 1978.

George Ewart Evans was a very sensitive, generous, and caring man, who wanted to help those who seemed to be always left out of things. It was important to him throughout his life. He used both fiction and documentary to portray the lives of working people.

The Voices of the Children is a work of fiction, but it breathes with a community's life and its nuanced behaviour. It is based firmly in the world of Evans' own childhood experiences of growing up in a large family in Abercynon, in the early years of the twentieth century. The language is as rhythmical as the knowledge expressed. It is a book full of the stories of childhood, the uncertainty and excitement that comes with growing up. But it also reveals with a child's honesty some of the received truths of the adult world.

I was glad I was not living in Mrs Wilkins' house. She had no children and spent nearly all the day cleaning and polishing. Her husband was a quiet man with a long neck, and she wore his trousers and his pants. He couldn't put a foot on the carpet in the house, and she'd hardly let him go upstairs to bed for fear of smudging the linoleum.

It will make you smile and it will make you laugh remembering the confusion of adolescence, and it will make you proud too, knowing how the ordinary people took the harshest of happenings and the most brutal of treatment in their stride.

At a very early age, George Ewart Evans was learning that work is not a chore but a duty to yourself and to others around you, and a way of getting to know your own worth.

Father said, 'There's an order for Penywaun. I want you to take the goods in the cart. David will go with you.'
Penywaun was a farm away up on the hog's-back of the hill about four miles out of the village. It was a tricky journey with a horse and cart, narrow mountain roads and a hill as steep as your forehead.

Even so, nowadays I'm always slightly amazed when people of my age end a conversation with, 'Mind you! I think we've had the best of times,' and I always agree. Leaving school at fourteen, out of bed at 5.45am, or stop lamp at 7.01am, seven and a half hours working on your knees, ready for bed by 9.30pm.

But the compensations are in the memories. Summer holidays spent whinberry picking on Blaen-pergwm, on the top of the mountain, more than an hour's walk from home and a mile from the nearest dwelling. A bottle of pop and sandwiches, and we would be away most of the day. Whilst these days, mothers and fathers fly into a blind panic if they lose sight of their child in their own street just for a moment.

Here is George Ewart Evans' reminder of those long ago days; carefree days when the boys go camping on Y Garth Fawr mountain.

> At dusk we carried the embers of the fire and placed them in the centre of the tent space, where they lit up the tent with a rich glow. We were eager to get inside the tent, to sit in a house we had built ourselves, around a hearth of our own making.

His biographer, Gareth Williams, wrote in the *Writers of Wales* volume on George Ewart Evans:

> Eventually it was oral history that, from the 1950s, became for George Ewart Evans a means of releasing that creativity as he developed a way of giving history back to the people in their own words. In recording the unforced rhythms and unadorned speech of his often unlettered informants, he believed he was restoring to the people a heightened sense of their own worth, making historic democratic activity.

I think it would please George Ewart Evans to know that, as one of those unlettered informants, I have been asked to write the foreword to *The Voices of the Children*, his first book, making a kind of unity of the oral and the written.

The novel clearly and lovingly illustrates what it was like to be born and grow up, not just in the valleys of South Wales but in an industrialized community, in the first forty years of the twentieth century.

George Brinley Evans

THE VOICES OF THE CHILDREN

PART I

My eldest sister had kept the fire in throughout the night, placing all the kettles and saucepans filled with water around it. Next morning she told us, 'You've got a new sister, but we haven't thought of a name for her yet.'

It was a Saturday and, since there was no school, I climbed over the wall at the back of the house into the dry bed of the canal to think about the new sister. How many was that? There were Tom and me and Arthur and David and then the girls and our Dinah and now the new one. That made how many? Oh, why were there so many children? But I should have known there another coming. Just before David came I saw the nurse in the house, and she'd been here again about a fortnight ago. What had the nurse to do with it? She didn't bring the baby, I was sure of that.

Someone was calling me, and I glanced up and saw my eldest sister looking over the wall.

'What are you doing down there? You know mother's in bed, and there's the milk to take round, and you have to take the horse's bridle to get it mended.'

'Oh, all right, I'm coming.'

I didn't mind my big sister, though, she had to be boss now and then, but she made up for it with a piece of chocolate, and best of all when I was in scrapes she always stood up for me and gave me a wink or a nudge as much as to say, 'Don't let it worry you; it's not so bad as they make it out to be.' She was dark, with big black eyes and hair the colour of a crow's wing. We called her Dinah. She didn't mind, although her proper name was Rachel. She could do anything in the house, make apple tart especially.

There were three regular customers for milk. We only had one cow, and we used most of the milk ourselves, selling only what was left over. I took the milk round in a gallon can with a half-pint measure hooked onto its handle. The first customer was Mrs Thomas, the teacher's wife. She was always dressed tidily, even in the morning. Her hair was in a net, and she spoke a little like the Cardiff people. As I poured out the milk into her jug she said, 'I hear you've got another sister. Has she got a name yet?'

I felt she had the knowing smile that everyone had when they asked about one of our new babies, or when they asked, 'How many is that in your family now?'

I bent over the milk and said, 'She hasn't a name yet.' I was ashamed that I was so confused. She looked at me with her eyes still smiling. I bent over again to pour out the extra drop of milk and, when I straightened up, my face was burning. As I climbed the hill to the next customer I asked myself with annoyance: why is it that I don't want there to be another baby? Why is it disgraceful to have such a big family? Disgraceful it was, I was sure of it.

Mrs Wilkins Checkweigher was bound to know about the new baby. She had her eye at the letter-box and knew everybody's business almost before it happened. When she opened the door she said with a chuckle, 'You've got another rival, eh!'

She was fat, and her apron belt, tied tightly round her middle, made her bulge out in two places like a big cottage-loaf. She shuffled round the door and thrust the jug in front of me.

I said politely, pretending I hadn't heard, 'Nice morning, Mrs Wilkins.'

She watched me intently as I poured out the two half pints of milk to see that I gave the full measure. 'Keep your hand steady now, or else you'll be spilling the milk on my clean doorstep. What's her name?'

I straightened up too quickly and spilled a drop of milk from the second measure. 'She hasn't got a name yet,' I said quickly, 'I haven't seen it either. It was born at three o'clock this morning and it's supposed to be like our Mary who's staying with my auntie in the country.'

'Oh,' she said, moving her feet back and looking at the doorstep. She was surprised at the flow of words, as I meant her to be. 'And how many does that make in your family now?'

I rattled the measure back onto the handle of the can

and made ready to go. 'Don't know. There's one more girl now at any rate.'

'Don't know! What do you mean? You don't know how many in your own family, boy! You ought to be proud of so many brothers and sisters. How many would there be? There's Rachel and Tom and you and David and Arthur and your two sisters staying with your auntie and the new one. Is there another?'

I picked up the can and started to walk towards the gate, edging out of the corner in which she'd pinned me. 'I'm in a hurry, Mrs Wilkins.'

She looked at me curiously, shaking her head as I escaped. But she suddenly became agitated, and just as I was going out through the gate she shouted loud enough for the whole street to hear, 'Wait a minute, you didn't give me my last measure full.'

I'd forgotten about the milk I'd spilled. As I poured out the extra drop she said, clicking her tongue, 'Well, well. You're a fine one. You in standard five – or is it six? – and don't know how many in your own family!'

I made my way quickly into the street. An empty tin was lying on the pavement and I gave it a kick, sending it flying over to the other side of the road. To hell with Mrs Checkweigher! May her garden never grow and may all her children have wooden legs!

On the way back I met Ginger Williams – he had a bucket and was collecting horse dung off the road. He waved his shovel and shouted, 'Finished the milk?'

I was glad to have someone to talk sense with, and I put the empty can down on the pavement and Ginger left his bucket and came across. He said, 'Fatty Hughes has had the football mended. We're going to have a game of sides up on the mountain this afternoon. Coming up?'

I quickly ran over my chances of a game that afternoon. What was there to do? Fetch the cow, chop the sticks, get coal and take out goods. Rashly I threw them all to the winds. 'Pick me, I'll come. What time are you starting?'

'We're meeting at two o'clock by Fatty's coalshed. Fourteen of us. No big 'uns.' Things were beginning to look much brighter. Then Ginger, looking at the toe of his boot, said, 'Saw the nurse coming out of your house this morning.'

I looked at him and nodded my head. (I may as well tell him, he probably knows anyway.) 'Ay, another baby.'

'Seen it yet?'

I shook my head. 'Heard it though. It's got a cry like fat frying, only louder, three times louder.'

Ginger nodded his head, frowning a little as he did when he was trying to think. He pulled two marbles out of his pocket. 'You can have this one,' he said as he handed me a shining glass taw. 'I know what you mean,' he went on as he breathed on the other marble. 'This is a good taw. Won sixteen off Dai Jeremiah. Does it hold its breath?'

'Yes,' I said, not without a little twist in the conscience, but I straightened it out thinking: all the others did, I expect this one does too. Ginger would understand; he liked new babies as much as I did. He once told me that all new babies were like little frogs, even the best looking of them.

As he put the marble back in his pocket he said with a wise look, 'When there's a new baby in the house the best

7

thing to do is go out and stay out. You don't hear it and you don't see the old women slobbering all over it.'

I could imagine Ginger stalking out with his hands in his pockets. That was the best thing to do.

A hoarse-voiced shouting broke up our talk. 'Get that bucket out of the road. Trying to kill my horse you are.'

We turned round and saw Jenkins the Milk prancing about in his float, and Ginger hurried to get the bucket, calling back as he left, 'Two o'clock by Fatty's coalshed.'

I went home feeling much better for my talk with Ginger, and after I'd taken the horse's bridle to the saddler's I went about the set jobs, keeping away from the shop to avoid any errands. I'd ask David to fetch the cow – he was getting old enough now. I thought, too, of asking for the afternoon off, going boldly up to Father and telling him where I wanted to go, but there was always the chance of a refusal and it was very important that day, as Ginger said, to go out and forget the new baby. Indeed, it gave me a reason for going. Besides, with the excitement in the house and people coming to ask how Mother was, I might not be missed. In the end I made up my mind to go without asking and, after deciding this, even a string of napkins across the line at the back of the house never disturbed me.

Later that morning Dinah took me up to see my mother. I didn't want to go but she shamed me into climbing the stairs and, when I was outside the bedroom, she pushed me forward, saying, 'Here he is. They've all been up to see you except him.'

Mother was sitting up in bed and she had a white woollen jacket on. Her black hair was all frizzed up in curls and she looked pretty, only she was very pale. She smiled at me and I didn't know which leg to put forward first. She said, 'Well, I thought you'd gone out to lodgings.'

I mumbled something and then Dinah nudged me from the back, 'Go on, you silly, aren't you going to ask Mother how she is?'

I said with great effort, 'Are you better, Mother?'

She nodded and, smiling at Dinah, she asked me, 'And don't you want to see your new sister?'

I noticed the cot for the first time. It was on the other side of the bed, with a blue coverlet spread over it. I kept trying to see which end the baby's head was, and I didn't notice that Dinah was leading me round the foot of the bed, I couldn't see any of the baby.

Dinah whispered, 'Don't make a noise, she's sleeping.'

We crept up to the side of the cot and Dinah pulled back the coverlet. I remembered Ginger's words, but I couldn't tell exactly whether it was like a frog, because even when the coverlet was pulled aside I could only see the top of its head, and that was as red as a bit of raw beef, and fine fluffy hair was all over it. But I wasn't curious to see if its face was like a frog, and I felt a sudden wish to get away and go and hide in the warehouse. I turned quickly to go out, but my foot caught the leg of the cot and there was a bang, followed by a squeal from the bundle in the cot, like a railway wagon pulling up with its brake on. The squeal got louder and louder, and the top of the head got redder and redder. I didn't wait for Dinah to say, 'Now look what you've done!' but I was off and out of the door and down the stairs in a rush. The noise sounded no better from the foot of the stairs but I heard Mother laughing, so it couldn't have been so serious as they pretended it to be.

My father kept a grocer's shop. It was at the bottom of the street near a crossroads, and a big chapel loomed up beside it like a cliff. Between the chapel and the yard of the shop was a wall, and clamped to the wall was a long ladder – too long and heavy to shift. Arthur and I had a look at it one day, and he said it was Jacob's ladder for reaching to Heaven, because if it were put on its end it would reach up a long way past the chapel or the big stack of the pit and even the mountain itself. We asked Davey Price the Painter about it and he said, 'Ay! Maybe it would reach to Heaven, only there's an easier way of getting there than climbing that ladder, bound to be.'

Davey ought to know, although he had never been anywhere near Heaven, it was he who had to climb the ladder when a gale blew the slates off the chapel roof.

Next to the shop was the house, and it was joined to the shop by two doors – one at the front and one at the back. Father and Mother used to live above the shop but, when the family began to grow, Father bought the house next door and knocked two holes in the wall to join it to the shop. In the back of the house he knocked down the wall dividing two rooms and made them into one big room where we could all sit down to meals together, and not have the meals in relays like they do at a Sunday school social. Over part of the big room there was a glass roof, and when it snowed the room became very dark, though it was easy to go upstairs to one of the bedrooms, open the window and, with a long broom, push the snow off the roof; or David, who was small and wiry, could put his slippers on and walk out a little way on the sloping roof while I held his jersey to steady him.

At the back of the big room there was a kitchen and a scullery, although the big room had a range and they did most of the cooking in there. On the other side was the middle room. Here there was a piano with a green silk cloth across it, pleated like an American shirt-front. The piano tinkled like bells when Dinah played it, and it made your ears tickle if you put your head against the back of it. Upstairs there were three bedrooms over the house and a bathroom with the keyhole stuffed with paper. The boys slept over the shop, where there were another two bedrooms – three really, because Tom and I slept in the paper-room. All round the walls of the paper-room there were shelves piled with bags and packing paper: blue, pink and yellow for sugar and fruit, and brown for ordinary packing. It was very cosy there because after the shop was shut we could have a game in bed without anyone hearing. Our Tom, who was the eldest, said it was a warm bedroom because the paper kept the cold out.

Next to the paper-room there was a storeroom full of canisters of coffee, sago, linseed, mixed spice, and peppercorns. On the floor were two coffee machines for grinding the coffee-berries. Tom did most of the coffee-grinding; he poured the berries into a funnel at the top and, when he turned the handle, a brown shower fell into the containers below and the room was full of the sweet scent of the berries.

There were two staircases, one leading to the little warehouse behind the shop. This staircase had no carpet on it and it was steep and we had to come down it quietly not to make a noise. The other staircase led up from the passage at the front door of the house and, since it had a carpet, the boys had to use the back staircase, but it was a good game to chase up one stairs and down the other.

Outside were the stables, the big warehouse, and the cart shed. There were two stalls in the stable: one for the horse and one for the cow. The cow's stall was the first one as you went in through the door, and her manger was level with the floor, while the horse's manger in the next stall was as high as my shoulder. For a long time I wondered why this was, for the horse seemed to have a longer neck than the cow. Then Arthur said one day, 'But can't you see, mun, the cow's got shorter legs.'

The cow's stall was pretty large, and we'd fixed up a swing from one of the rafters, and when the cow was out grazing we could swing for a whole afternoon.

Joined to the stable, and forming the long arm of a letter 'L', was the big warehouse. There were two storeys to it and you reached the second storey by opening a trapdoor and putting a ladder through it. In the loft, on one side of the trapdoor, the hay for the horse and cow was kept; on the other were sacks of potatoes and corn for the shop. In between there was a chaff-cutter for making chaff of the hay, and a slicer for cutting up mangel-wurzels for the cow. There wasn't a finer place for spending a wet afternoon. Underneath, on the ground floor, were bins and sacks of meal and corn and a weighing machine, and at one end were two long stone slabs like tables. These were for salting bacon. We could put two pigs down to salt at the same time. Under the slabs were two tubs for pickling.

In the cartshed next to the warehouse there was a business cart for taking out the goods, and also a pleasure trap for Sundays and holidays. The trap had yellow wheels with thin black lines and its body was black with thin yellow lines. We could fix two seats in the trap. They stretched from side to side and faced in opposite directions. Father and Mother always sat in the front with the baby and three of us were squeezed tight in the back, tied to the seat with straps buckled round our waists to stop us from getting left behind. Our legs were covered up with a rug, and it was fine sitting in the back to see the things come suddenly from the side, and the road unwinding underneath the tail-board like a long grey ribbon. But we couldn't put all the family in the trap, not by half, and there was always a big competition for places.

I came in from the football a little disturbed; now that I was back, the game seemed a small pleasure to balance the row there'd be if I'd been missed. I ducked under the back window of the shop and went into the stable. The cow was in her stall – David must have brought her in – but I could see by the way she was looking round that she hadn't been fed. She gave a deep sigh as I went into the boxroom behind her stall and took a bucketful of meal from one of the bins.

After I'd mixed her mash and cut a few mangel-wurzels for her, I noticed a drop of milk coming from her udder. She hadn't been milked! Tom was out with the cart delivering goods and he was later than usual. I had a sudden idea: if I milked the cow everybody would be so surprised and pleased that they would forget I'd been missing in the afternoon. I went straightway to the scullery and took the enamel milking-pail down off the shelf. I found the milking-stool and soon had my head in Daisy's side with the bucket tilted between my knees and the milk bouncing against the bottom of the empty pail. But it didn't bounce for long; in less than two minutes my wrists felt as if they were tightly bound with bands of lead. They felt lighter after I'd rested them, but as soon as I started again I seemed to lose all feeling in them. There was no grip in my hands, and instead of closing them gently I began to jerk and pull the udder. The cow knew what was happening and didn't like it; she began edging away to the other side of the stall, and I had to follow after her, stumbling with the stool and the bucket. At last she reached the wall and couldn't edge away any farther, but then she began to use her tail: I felt a sharp pain across my face as the tail curled around my head. Each time I pulled at the udder the tail came round like a whip, stinging my face as much as a piece of elastic flicked against it. I straightened up and spoke to the cow in Welsh – she could understand Welsh better than English, although she was a Hereford – and as soon as I stopped pulling at her she became still, but when I started again the tail swung like a flail.

Then David strolled out with his hands in his pockets just as I was about to give it up. He said, 'What are you up to?'

'Hold her tail, Nipper. Tight. I'm having a go at milking her.'

He leaned over the pail. 'How much have you got?'

The bottom of the pail was barely covered with milk. He looked at me and kept silent.

'Did they miss me this afternoon?'

'I don't think so. There've been people to see the new baby.'

Good for the new baby! And Nipper was a good fellow, too, for covering up. I attacked the cow with new hope, but immediately the tail began to work again and, *whish!* out of Nipper's hand it came and the side of my face was smarting.

'Hold it with two hands, Nipper.'

I was getting determined now, and I gave Daisy a push with the heel of my hand and spoke a few sharp words to her. She just looked round mildly.

Then Nipper had an idea. 'Give her some mangels.'

He got a few pieces out of the bucket and placed them in her manger, but she wouldn't look at them whilst I sat by her – bribery was not going to help. I took to the udder again and set to work while Nipper held her tail gently with both hands. 'It will be all right once you start it running,' he said.

'It isn't a tap, mun. It's easy to start, to keep it running is the thing. Hold the tail, boyo. Here goes.'

For a few seconds the milk made music at the bottom of the pail, and then there was a sudden upheaval and the stall seemed to tilt on one of its sides. Somehow the pail was snatched from between my knees and I fell back, finishing up against the other side of the stall.

When I got up, Nipper, who was laughing too much to speak, kept pointing at the bucket, and each time he pointed he went off into further spurts of laughter. The bucket was still upright, but one of the cow's back legs sprouted out of it like a tree out of a garden-tub. I jumped up to catch at the handle without stopping to think. 'Stop your laughing now, and give us a hand.'

Nipper held the pail while I tried to lift the leg. I failed. I put my shoulder against it and I pushed. Nothing happened; the more we struggled, the more solidly did the foot press down. As we paused for breath, I could hear the quiet tinkle of the enamel cracking in the pail. The old cow was looking to the front as unconcerned as if it were all a part of each day's happenings.

Nipper said, 'We'll never lift her leg out of it.'

'No, we'll have to push her over to the other side of the stall. It doesn't matter if it tips now.' I gave an anxious glance out through the door and then I said, 'Righto, Nip.'

We both put our hands on her haunches and pushed. After a bit of straining and shouting, she moved languidly right over to the other side of the stall, lifting her leg out of the pail at the last moment without even touching its sides.

The milk was a dirty greyish-green. I picked up the pail and quickly emptied it down the drain. 'Wash the stall down with some water, Nip, while I clean this pail.'

I ran into the scullery and scalded the pail with hot water. There was no black patch in the enamel as I expected, but as I lifted it up to replace it on the shelf I heard the cracking still going on inside like an echo.

16

When I returned, everything in the stall was quiet: Daisy was eating the mangels, and Nipper was leaning against the partition of the stalls, and there was no sign of the struggle.

Tom came in very soon afterwards, whistling as usual. He was very tall and had a red face and could lift Nipper up into the loft with one arm. He looked into the stall and his eye caught Nipper's and he asked, 'What have you lads been up to?'

Nipper thrust his hands more deeply into his pockets and looked at me with a grin, but I said quickly to Tom, 'You're a bit late tonight, Tom. We'll unharness the horse and feed him while you're milking, if you like.'

Nipper was still grinning, and Tom caught him by the collar and the seat of the pants and lifted him onto the cow's back. He said, '*Dere fuwch*,' in a deep voice and the cow never even flicked her tail. 'Righto, see to the horse. And you can take the boxes out of the cart – we'll be finished in no time. Get the pail first, Nipper.' He lifted him down and in half a minute the milk was flowing in a white stream into the pail.

We watched a while, fascinated as we listened to the steady swish of the flow. Nipper looked at me and said in a whisper, 'See how it's done?'

Tom heard him and turned his head slightly and a certain look came into his eyes. Then with a turn of the wrist he sent a thin fountain of milk pencilling towards us, but we had both seen the look before: we ducked while the milk made a pattern on the half-door behind us.

When we had stalled the horse and fed him and laid down the bedding of crinkly bracken, we went in to see

17

Tom's bucket of milk standing covered with fine thin gauze.

'Not so much as usual,' he said while we looked at it. Then Nipper laughed again, and Tom grabbed him as he tried to back away. 'C'mon, out with it. What have you been up to?'

Nipper said, 'Nothing, nothing!' but before the evening was out we told Tom what had happened and he said, 'Well, you're a handy pair, but there's no harm done. I'll teach you to milk – the both of you.'

Since it was Sunday morning everybody had a half hour extra in bed. The shop was closed and there was no need to get up till much later. Arthur and I lit the fire – Arthur was between Nipper and me. When he was a baby, a traveller coming to the shop told my mother, 'He's long-headed; he'll be a fast one at school.' Arthur was a great reader.

As I came downstairs on Sundays I had to ask myself, 'Which is it to be this morning: go to chapel, or stay at home and peel the potatoes?' The chapel seats were very hard and the service took a long time, and a bucket full of potatoes took a lot of peeling. It wasn't an easy thing to choose between them. If Arthur and I hadn't made our choice by ten o'clock, Dinah decided how we were to spend our morning. This Sunday she said to me, 'You go to chapel – you and David. You haven't been on a Sunday morning for over a month.'

She was right – I'd peeled the potatoes for four weeks running. A fortnight before I'd taken a cutting from the paper. It said that it was much better to boil potatoes in their jackets as all the goodness was just under the skin. Dinah had read the cutting and had shown it to Mother, who said, 'We'll try it.' But Dinah said to me, 'Don't think you'll have nothing to do. You'll have to scrub them hard with a scrubbing brush, and rinse them three times.'

Well, I scrubbed the potatoes hard, and I rinsed them four times to make sure and still I'd only taken half as long as if I'd peeled them. It was a great discovery and a whole line of pleasant Sunday mornings opened out before me. But before dinner was over that day I knew my scheme had gone wrong. As soon as the dish of potatoes came to the table they all turned up their noses. Arthur said, 'I don't like the colour. They look like stones.' Father said, 'They taste earthy – boiled like this in their skins,' and Nipper asked, 'Where's the potatoes?'

Although I showed them the cutting, which I still kept under the china dog on the mantel-shelf, it was no use, they didn't want vitamins and I knew that on the following Sunday it would be peeled again.

The family had a pew in the chapel and it was understood that, whenever there was a service there, the pew was never to be empty; someone had to go to 'represent the family'. Nipper and I were going this morning. We changed into our best clothes as slowly as we could. Nipper couldn't find his socks, and we were doing well until Dinah shouted up the stairs, 'Look in his best boots, and hurry up or else I'll be up there to help you.' And when I lost my stud she pounced on one in a drawer in the big dresser in the living-room and had a collar round my neck before I could draw breath, and was telling me to go back and wash behind my ears as well.

We were ready by half past ten and then she said to us, 'You've got the book. No antics now and don't shuffle with your feet. Go on now, they've just begun the first hymn.'

A thin melancholy chorus came from the chapel with Evan Davies the Deacon's voice climbing above the others. At the last moment Nipper found that he hadn't a handkerchief, and they were singing the last verse of the hymn before Dinah led us out of the yard on our way to chapel. As we were leaving she whispered to me, 'Take these for when you get tired,' and she slipped a small packet of Minto sweets into my hand, though she came to the side door of the yard to see that we went into the chapel and didn't dodge round the corner and off to the canal bank and on to the mountain.

The small porch of the chapel was full of late comers. Mrs Wilkins Checkweigher was next to the door talking to a thin little woman with glasses. She leaned over her, whispering violently, creasing her face up and moving her head as quickly as a chicken pecking. The little woman stared at her, but I couldn't see her eyes because the light shone on her glasses.

Watkins the Tailor was at the door and, just as they were singing the last two lines, he peeped in and raised his hand for everyone in the porch to stop talking. Mrs Wilkins' face set as hard as the face on a china jug and, after Watkins had peeped in once more, he opened the door and she went in first, sailing up the aisle to the front pew, the feather in her hat leading.

Mr Ebenezer the Preacher stood up straight in the pulpit

watching the procession of latecomers. He had one hand on the book and the other under the tail of his long coat, and we could see by his face that he was going to say a 'little word' about getting up on a Sunday morning.

Mr Ebenezer was tall and he had a deep, rolling voice. When he was in his *hwyl* the people at the top of John Street could hear him, and when he banged the pulpit with his fist we could feel the floor of the chapel quiver. Before he went to the Baptist College he was a good rugby forward and Jack Ragtime used to say that it was a good job for Beynon the Policeman that Dick Ebenezer went for a minister, because if he hadn't it would have taken six of Beynon's sort to throw him out of a public house on a Saturday night.

When Watkins the Tailor had closed the door, the preacher opened the book to read, and his voice rumbled round the chapel and his words got into my belly. If ever I imagine God, two pictures of him come into my mind: one is a stern, bearded man sitting upright on the Big Throne, a long white robe flowing over him and a bare big toe sticking out from underneath it, and a black book with gilt clasps is on his knee; in the other picture he's in his working clothes and he's dressed like Mr Ebenezer the Preacher – all in black, with a long jacket reaching down to his knees and a wide black hat, his deep collar starched like his front, with a black bow across it. He stands up straight and looks at the world from under bushy eyebrows and when he opens his mouth the people tremble.

Mr Ebenezer had God's look and his secret voice of thunder. If a boy fidgeted in his pew, he stopped his reading

21

and glanced up, and it was much better for that boy to bury his head and crawl under the pew out of sight, than to meet the preacher's gaze or hear the anger in his voice.

Another stream of very late ones came in after he had finished reading, and they were glad that he was sitting down in the pulpit out of sight. After they had all got to their pews the third hymn started, and the singing now had a little more body in it. Davies the Deacon led, keeping time with his book and singing a bit smaller than he did in the first hymn.

They sang the last two lines of the hymn twice only. Davies could usually tell if there was any feeling in the chapel and if they wanted it three times. But Nipper and I always kept our eyes on Johnny Cantwr, an old husk of a man in the corner. He liked to go off on his own and, when everybody else – having taken their cue from Davies – had sat down, Johnny would often be on his feet starting to pipe the lines again, and then we'd all have to stand up once more to help him out with his solo. But this morning he wasn't in voice and sat down before Davies the Deacon, and the congregation settled down thankfully.

Mr Ebenezer then prayed with his face screwed up and his hands stretched out before him. Then came the collection, when everyone had a chance to see who was in the chapel and who'd be likely to have all the news when they got outside.

Before the sermon itself, we had a hymn with three tails and the preacher opened the book again and read a verse. His voice was low and even. He was always quiet at the beginning – not that he really warmed up on a Sunday morning: it was only a canter, a try-out, for the evening. Nipper and I listened to the preacher for a while and watched him whip out his white handkerchief from a secret pocket in the tail of his jacket, and then we ate the sweets and made a mouse out of our handkerchiefs. When we were tired of this, we looked at the preacher but our thoughts were coursing over the coming week.

I came back to the sermon very suddenly when the preacher shouted out – his voice took hold of me like a strong wind. From then on I had to listen. His face was red and his eyes shone with fire and his voice, at one moment, was a trumpet of brass; at the next, a soft whisper of silver. He became quiet after a while and then we saw him act. It was better than the pictures: he was showing how Samuel was climbing the steps of the temple – a small boy lifting his knees high, and slowly mounting the huge steps, to clean the chambers of the Lord. He got down from the pulpit and stood on a level with the Big Seat. Before he climbed the first step, he shrank to a small boy; we could only see his head over the handrail – he was a small boy. As he climbed he spoke in a quiet sing-song helping his acting with his words; the weary words of a boy going to an uninteresting task, mounting the steps slowly and unwillingly. He got halfway and he looked back as if he would return, but he pushed on, half complaining, half resigned. He climbed higher and higher the steep steps of the temple, and with a final urge he reached the top and stood ready to face the High Priest. A small boy who had won his battle. It was then I had a shock that made me grip the seat, for Mr Ebenezer was still in the pulpit and not somewhere up under the roof as he should have been.

After the last hymn Nipper and I couldn't get down the aisle quickly enough. The people gathered in groups outside the chapel and we took a look round at the morning and decided to visit Mrs Llewellyn who lived up in John Street – we couldn't go looking for nests in our best clothes. Mrs Llewellyn was a good customer in the shop. Her husband was troubled with nystagmus, through working in the pit and he was always glad of someone to talk to.

On the way up the street we met Ginger Williams – he never went to chapel on a Sunday morning. He was walking with his father and had a little terrier on the lead. As they passed he stopped and whispered to us, 'My Dad's got a ferret in his pocket. We've had some sport. The bitch has caught five rats this morning.' Then he went cantering after his father and left Nipper and me thinking how dull is holiness, and how exciting is the path of the wicked!

We went into Mrs Llewellyn's through the back door. Mr Llewellyn sat on a high-backed settle near the fire, his walking stick between his legs and on his head a cap. He always wore a soft cap, even when he was sitting by the fire. He was a mild little man with a beard. As soon as he heard our footsteps he called out, 'Come in, boys. Who is it this morning, David and Arthur?'

'No. David and Willie.'

'Lizzie,' he called out, 'here's the boys.'

Mrs Llewellyn came from the front of the house and pushed the teapot nearer the fire. She was a grey-haired woman with a shiny red face and was as kind as another auntie. She gave us each a cup of tea and a piece of cake and then went back to her job saying, 'I'll be back in ten minutes. Don't go; stay and have a chat with Mr Llewellyn till I come back.'

After a silence, when we both looked at the unseeing eyes of the old man, I said, 'We've got a new pair of reins for the horse – the others kept breaking.'

And Nipper joined in, 'The new ones are brown leather. But we shall put black oil on them to make them the same colour as the rest of the harness.'

It was strange talking to the old man, because you couldn't see from his eyes what he was thinking. But he was a kind old man. He seemed to take the things we told him into his brain and let them run round and round there until he had seen all their paces, and then he would say suddenly, as though he approved of them, 'Yes. That's right. That's quite right.' And this was such a long time afterwards that you wondered whether he was seeing other things in his mind and not the ones you were talking about.

He turned his head very slightly and we heard someone coming down the stairs. Jack Ragtime had just got up. He came into the kitchen in his stockinged feet, carrying his boots in one hand and his watch and chain in the other.

Jack Ragtime was Mrs Llewellyn's lodger, and got out of bed when he liked. He was a big, square man just come back from the war. They called him Ragtime because he was always singing. Sometimes, too, in the pit he would recite *The Shooting of Dan Magrew* and they all stopped work to hear him. He winked at us as he sat down at the table, and began to wind his watch.

Mrs Llewellyn came in and got him his breakfast, asking

him with a lift of her voice, 'You're sure it's breakfast you want and not dinner?'

He grinned at us as Mrs Llewellyn went out, and then began to eat his breakfast.

Before he buttered his bread, he warmed the knife in his tea. He noticed us watching him and said, 'Don't let your mother catch you doing that. Bad habit isn't it, Dad?'

The old man answered in his serious voice, 'That's right, *bach*,' and Nipper looked at him quickly, wondering how he could see.

'Ay,' Ragtime went on, 'that's the sort of thing you pick up in the army. A rough old gang in the army.'

I asked him, 'Did you see any Germans when you were in the army?'

He stopped chewing and put down his knife. 'Germans! *Duw*. Thousands of 'em. Even the Kaiser himself.' He looked at us shrewdly and saw the interest in our faces. 'Didn't I ever tell you that I met the Kaiser?' He took a gulp of tea and pushed his chair away from the table. He filled his pipe slowly and, by the time he had finished, our attention was all his.

'Well! It was just like this: just after we crossed the Rhine about seventeen months ago, we ran into the Kaiser himself – me and another chap named Dai Roderick from Treorchy. He was taking his dog for a walk, just the same as you or me would be taking our whippet for an airing along by the bank of the Taff there on a Sunday morning. As soon as he saw me he stopped and said, "Hello, Ragtime. I didn't expect to see you here so soon," and I said to him, "*Sut mae*, Bill, and I didn't expect to see you neither. This is Dai Roderick from the Rhondda." He shook hands with Dai and was quite friendly, but I could see he was a bit down in the mouth, and I said to him looking at the dog, "Is he any good for ratting, Bill?" And he shook his head and said, "Good for nothing, pal." The poor old dog did look sorry for himself indeed, with his tail right down between his short back legs. So to cheer the both of them up a bit I said, "Coming along our way for a stroll?" But he got more dismal still and said, "I'm sorry, Jack, it can't be done. It's like this: you move in and I move out." Then he brightened up a bit and said briskly, "Here, hold the dog a minute." So I took the lead, not that there was any danger of the old dog going off – he didn't have enough go in him to lie down – and the Kaiser started searching in his pockets until at last he found a small scissors. Then he said, "Jack, I can't come with you, but before I go I'll give you something to remember me by." And *snip!* before we knew it, off came a big piece of his moustache and he was holding it out to me saying with a catch in his voice, "Keep this in your locket, Jack, and remember your old pal Bill." Then he walked on slowly up the river bank dragging his dog behind him, and I never saw him again except in his photo, and that was in a pub down in Ponty where they were swilling him with the bottom of the beer mugs.'

He paused and shook his head as though he were living the sad scene over again. 'But I've got the bit of moustache here in my wallet, haven't I, Dad?' He began searching his pockets. 'No, it's in my coat. No,' then he shouted out, 'Missus, bring the wallet down from under my pillow will you? You know, the one with the locket.'

Mrs Llewellyn called back from the top of the stairs, 'Wallet! What wallet? Go on with you, *bychan*! You haven't got a wallet, you know that. You lost it that night you came home without your jacket.'

Ragtime stirred his tea thoughtfully. 'Ay, so I did. So I did. Well, I can't show it to you after all, boys. But I must get Dai Roderick over to...'

We both laughed outright and Nipper said, 'Show us the tattoo on your chest instead.'

He looked at Nipper from the corner of his eye and, getting up from the table, suddenly lunged at him and caught him by his coat collar. Then holding the seat of his pants, he lifted him off the chair and held him up until his back was touching the ceiling – Nipper was small and perky and everyone wanted to hoist him up. 'Who told you I got a lady on my chest? Where's that hook, Missus? The one you hang the bacon on?'

He kept circling round with Nipper on his extended arm, calling out till Mrs Llewellyn came running in. She stopped and raised her arms when she saw what was happening. 'Put him down, Jack, *bach*. Put him down. Quick, he's got his best trousers and coat on.'

He placed Nipper back on the chair as gently as an egg on a shelf. Nipper was still grinning, 'I don't believe you've got a lady on your chest!'

'All right, come up when I'm having a tub.'

We saw by the clock that it was time for dinner and, since on a Sunday everybody had to be at the table before dinner started, we left and hurried home. The dinner wasn't quite ready, but Arthur was sitting at the table with his knife and fork in his hands.

Arthur was plump and was always prompt at meal times. He was saying, 'I'm hungry, our Dinah. If dinner's not going to be ready for another ten minutes, do you think I could have a piece of bread-and-butter to go on with?'

It was hard to refuse Arthur, because he could always ask so neatly. But Dinah, leaning over the range stirring the gravy, pretended not to hear him. Yet Arthur had learned the force of words: 'The dinner is late, our Dinah. It was ready at half-past twelve last Sunday, and now it's nearly five to one. We had breakfast at quarter to eight and, after all, I did do the potatoes. A piece of bread-and-butter won't spoil my dinner; all this waiting will spoil it.'

Dinah stood up and poured the gravy into a tureen, saying coolly, 'You wait, my lad, the dinner will be ready before you can count your fingers.'

Arthur put down his knife and fork and looked dismally at his hands.

Nipper said, 'He can't count. He'd have to wait till tea-time before he got his dinner.'

Dinah turned her back to the fireplace to hide her face. Arthur was still looking at his hands with disgust. 'Go on, count them!' Then he began telling off his fingers.

'That's my thumb. That's the finger I cut with the chopper. That's the finger I do the top button of my shirt up with. That's the finger next to the little finger, and I can play one of the black notes on the piano with that. And that's my little finger. What can I do with my little finger? I can make a fox's head in shadow and the little finger is his bottom jaw.'

'Show us.'

'I'll show you tonight when we've got a candle in the bedroom.'

We were sitting in our places and had all forgotten we were so hungry. Dinah, laughing outright now, said, 'No more now. Here it is, ready. Fetch a jug of water, David; and, Willie, call the others. Then we'll start.'

Father, who had been writing letters in the shop, was the last to come to the table, and after he had sat down and carved, there was silence in the house except for 'More please,' and the merry clatter of plates.

Uncle Tom called to see the baby. Uncle Tom was old, although he was still working in the pit down at Pontygwaith. He was my father's uncle really. His father had been a schoolmaster in the village where he and my grandmother were born. He had learned from his father how to write copperplate and how to print with a goose feather. Once, he engraved Tom's name on a penknife, as clever as a machine. When I asked him how he did it, he winked his eye and moved his chin up and down as though he were brushing it with his huge white moustache. 'Aqua fortis, my boy. Aqua fortis! Water that's strong. You'll get it at any good chemist.'

If anything pleased him greatly he said, 'Aqua fortis, Aqua fortis!' with much feeling. It was like the cobbler's leather to him. He could inscribe a verse in a book, too, so that one could hardly tell it from printing. He wrote a verse in Dinah's book starting, 'Be good sweet maid, and let who can be clever...' but Dinah was annoyed and called him a big old hypocrite, though Uncle Tom laughed and drew his hand over his moustache and tried to pat Dinah on the shoulder. She slipped away and said he was an old fool. Indeed, he did seem to have more lark in him than many men half his age. He was as thin as a spindle and as active on his feet as a billy goat.

We heard somebody knocking at the front door of the house and Dinah said, 'I'd better go. It may be the nurse.'

She went to the front and Nipper and I, who happened to be in the middle room, peeped along the passage to see who it was. When she opened the door there was nothing to see except Mrs Lewis Opposite's curtains, so she stepped out to look along the street. As she put her foot on the doorstep, someone jumped with a shout from the side. But Dinah was too cool and clever to be frightened, and she stepped back straight away and slammed the door so hard that it made white dust come down from the ceiling. Then she turned round and her eyes were bright and angry, though she smiled when she saw us watching. 'If he wants to come in, he can come in through the yard round the back way, the old rodney!'

We had both seen the bristling white moustache and had recognised Uncle Tom. Nipper said, 'He may be laid out on the pavement,' but Dinah wasn't alarmed.

'It would serve him right if he was. But the door didn't hit him – he was too quick, the monkey! Wait a few minutes. He'll soon be here, finding his way in, as certain as bad news.'

We waited in the living-room. Dinah was ironing as if nothing had happened and Nipper was searching in a drawer for a top, while I was pretending to do my homework. After a few minutes there were light footsteps in the yard outside, and then we heard Uncle Tom's voice, well controlled in a high sing-song, '*Ble mae'r bobl 'ma?* Where's the people here? Anybody at home?'

We saw the moustache for the second time and then he pranced round the door with his head thrust forward. Dinah didn't move, not even a turn of the head towards him. He slipped from one foot to the other, looking round and winking at Nipper and me. 'Well, there's a welcome to give your relation.'

Dinah held the iron off the garment and said without turning round, 'Ssh! Not so loud, please.'

'Where's the new baby then? Let's have a look at him.'

But Dinah didn't answer at once; she folded the garment and then turned and said coldly, 'To begin with it's not a "him", and if you want to see the baby you must act like a man in his proper senses.'

It was no good rating Uncle Tom, he only kept fooling the more. 'Come, come, Rachel. Too many napkins to wash, eh?'

'It's a pity you haven't got something better to do at your age than fool round like a schoolboy.'

Uncle Tom sighed as deeply as the suction fan in the pit, and then moved across to the fireplace behind Dinah, to stand with his back to the fire. For a few moments he was quiet. The ticking of the clock and the swish of the iron seemed to soothe him, and he turned and looked thoughtfully into the fire, his hands in his pockets and his feet apart. For an instant he looked an old man, but he quickly straightened himself up and said in his old, brisk voice, 'There's hospitality for you now. Aren't you going to ask an old fellow to put his bones down on a chair or something?'

He moved over towards the sofa, but Dinah still kept on with the ironing. She was determined to put Uncle Tom in his place and keep him there. And now was her chance since, for the time, she was mistress in the house.

Uncle Tom prepared to sit down, giving the ironing a keen glance before trying another sally. He sighed again with great emphasis and put his hands on his knees. Then something made Dinah look up: Uncle Tom was just settling himself down on the sofa; his head was forward and his thin legs were bent as he was about to heave his weight onto the cushions of the sofa. Dinah straightened up like a spring and the iron crashed to the table and she gave a scream which made Uncle Tom jump back to the hearth rug like a scalded cat. She said weakly, 'Oh, the baby! The baby! You would have killed her.'

A small white bundle on the sofa began to send out a wail – a continuous note with painful gaps as it broke. Dinah looked at Uncle Tom with an anxious face. 'Did you touch her? Oh!' She took the bundle and held it over her shoulder, patting it with her hand and swaying from one foot to the other.

Uncle Tom looked at her sheepishly and, as the row went on, he raised his hands above his head and said, 'Well, well, well. What a rumpus!' Then he looked round for a retreat and, seeing us, he called, 'Come on out, *bechgen i*, and show me the animals!'

The horse and the cow were in the stables. The cow was chewing the cud and gave a low bellow when we went in.

She looked round when Uncle Tom patted her on the back and the chain round her neck rattled as it slid up the bar.

'Easy, old gel. Does she still milk as good as ever?'

The horse heard this strange voice and his foot clanged on the stone floor of his stall. Nipper climbed up on the partition between the two stalls and patted him on the back, saying, 'Whoa, Dick,' but he still clattered, causing Uncle Tom to say, 'Well, well, the animals are as restless as the baby!'

His moustache moved up and down; he was studying the cow with interest. Although he had worked so long in the pits, he'd never forgotten the farm life in the village where he had spent his boyhood. He said with half-closed eyes, 'There's a clean smell in a stable that's better than the stale sour smell of the pit. The old pit is an invention of the Devil and it's got his smell about it – singed air and sulphur.'

When he cursed the pit we knew he would talk of his life in the village, but footsteps in the yard outside interrupted the flow of his thoughts. When we looked over the half-door of the stable we saw Arthur and Davies the Blacksmith. Davies was coming to shoe the horse. He had his canvas bag with his tools and the shoes which he had already made in the smithy. He was a blacksmith in one of the pits and did our horse in his spare time. We looked forward to Davies the Blacksmith's visit because, although we didn't see him work the bellows, shoeing the horse was always a sight we made sure not to miss.

Uncle Tom greeted him. 'Well, John Davies, and how are you? I haven't seen you since last big meeting!'

Mr Davies put down his bag slowly and shook hands with Uncle Tom. He was short and as broad as a door and had a pipe in his mouth at all times. 'Big meeting you said, Tom Pritchard? Which big meeting was that? Not this year's or the one before that. It's ages since I saw you in the chapel. But how are things in the Daran?'

'Oh, they still got some coal down there. You're working overtime.'

Davies nodded as he opened the door to the horse's stall. 'Pony all right?' he asked me.

I respected a man who called Dick a pony – he was certain to know horses and ponies from their manes to the tips of their tails. Dick knew who it was as soon as he heard Davies' voice, and stopped his shuffling about and stood up as still as a fair-horse. Mr Davies opened the canvas bag with his tools on the floor of the stall and asked me to get a light. It was getting dark outside and there was only one small grating high up in the wall of Dick's stall. I brought the hurricane lamp and two candles as well, so that he'd be certain to see the nails. We lit the candles and placed them high up on the ledge of the partition between the two stalls, and the white lime on the walls reflected the light, making the stable as bright as the window of a shop.

We shut the top half of the outside door and the three of us – Nipper, Arthur and I – climbed up on the ledge to watch. Uncle Tom stood at the back of the stall, sucking his pipe and talking to Mr Davies as he worked. The cow lay down on the bedding, and her breath rose in a thin steam that made the stall smell sweet and healthy.

The stable was a cosy place at night. The animals soon

drove the cold out of the small building, and when we lit the hurricane lamp and sometimes another oil lamp it was almost as warm as the living-room. It was strange, and restful, too. The shadows cast by the lamps on the white walls could be made at will into monsters or a grotesque fantastic procession, made alive by a gentle swing of the lamp.

The quiet movements of the animals drove away all loneliness. Here was the best place to talk or have a yarn, a secret place and, sometimes, after Tom had finished, a pal of his came in and we listened to stories of a bigger world, horseshows and fights and army life, until Tom said, 'It's getting late. Inside, you kids, and get your supper!'

We watched Davies bending his strength over the hoof, taking out the old nails with his sharp pincers, levelling off the horn; fitting the new shoe, nailing it and paring the hoof with his curved knife and filing it when he had finished. He worked quickly and smoothly, speaking to the pony in a language he could understand. It was all so interesting that I hardly breathed and my mouth got dry through watching. Davies straightened up occasionally to answer Uncle Tom's questions – they were talking about the pits – or to give his opinion, and it was only then that we became aware of what he was saying. While the blacksmith worked, all our interest was on his movements; the dull blow of the hammer on the nail as it was driven home, the rasp of the file, and the knife showing the mottled whiteness of the hoof.

At last it was over, and Davies gave Dick a friendly slap on the back for his patient standing, and then he gathered up his tools in his canvas bag. Uncle Tom offered him his tobacco pouch and, after there was a good cloud of smoke crouching under the ceiling, they settled down to do the real talking, and for us it was only the minutest shift of our interest.

Uncle Tom asked, 'How long have you been down in the Daran, John?'

'Since they started. I was there when they were sinking. That's twenty-three years ago.' The blacksmith blew out a cloud of smoke and said proudly, 'If I had as many pounds as I've shoed horses down in that pit, I wouldn't be talking to you here now, Twm.'

Uncle Tom's moustache bristled up and down, 'And where would you be then, in the name of prophets?'

John Davies took his pipe out of his mouth and gave this long thought, then he shrugged his shoulders as if it didn't matter very much where he liked to be, as long as he really didn't have the means to be any other place than where he was at present. 'Oh, I'd be on top of the mountain with a little terrier, like as not, catching a few rabbits or rooting out a rat.'

Uncle Tom gave a chuckle. 'You wouldn't spend many of your pounds that way, John. I thought at least you'd be buying a motor car and living in Llandaff, in a house with venetian blinds, with the electric light always left on in the passage.'

John Davies shook his head. 'Not for me, Twm. I always stick to the Valleys. I've burrowed in now like an old badger, and it will take a lot of digging to get me out.'

'That's right, *bychan*. Quite right, indeed. The old Valleys have got something flying about in them besides the coal dust.'

John Davies nodded his head and grunted. For a moment there was silence, then he said out of a cloud of smoke, 'You remember how we used to take the terriers down on a Sunday sometimes, to catch rats?'

'Ay, I've taken a terrier down myself.'

'I had the finest ratter in the Three Valleys. He'd go down on a Sunday morning and he wouldn't come up until he'd caught his twenty. He was afraid of the pit – going down in the cage you had to nurse him like a baby – but once he was down, you couldn't hold him.'

Uncle Tom smoked his pipe and nodded silently as John Davies lost himself in the past. 'A most peculiar thing, Tom Pritchard, happened with that terrier. A most peculiar thing! We were down one Sunday – the terrier, Dan Dowlais, and myself. You remember Dan Dowlais, the chap whose brother was carrying on with a black woman down in Cardiff there?'

Uncle Tom chuckled. 'Ay, I remember Dan Dowlais. That same brother was supposed to have a big position in the Portuguese Navy, but that's another story. Go on, John.'

'Well, we'd been at it with the rats for the best part of the morning, and just when we were starting back we spotted a beauty right on the parting where they'd started to drive a new heading; down where Wil Cochyn's is now. Now this rat wasn't the same colour as the others. It was lighter, much lighter. I'm not saying it was a white rat, mind you, but just lighter. Lighter! You could pick it out from other rats with half an eye. Well, when we saw this rat, a funny thing happened: it didn't move; it just stopped in the middle of the roadway and looked. And the terrier stopped dead about three yards away from it. The terrier looked at the rat and then looked at Dan Dowlais and me, but we couldn't get our eyes off the rat, it was staring at us solid, with the light from our lamps catching its eyes. The terrier bristled up like a hedgehog. Although he was frightened, he was just going in after him, I could tell that, when *crash!* down came about six tons of top not two yards from where we were standing. When most of the dust had cleared off, we saw that the terrier was safe; there was nothing to be seen of the rat.'

He paused and re-lit his pipe, and Uncle Tom puffed quietly, standing with one foot thrust out in front of the other as though he was in deep thought. John Davies went on. 'The terrier was safe, but as true as I'm standing here talking to you now, that terrier would never so much as look at a rat after that. He could meet a rat in a drainpipe and he'd let it go by him like a puppy. A most peculiar thing, Tom Pritchard, and it would take a better man than me to explain it.'

Uncle Tom still smoked, shaking his head slowly, but we couldn't tell whether he was disbelieving or merely puzzled. So John Davies had to tell another peculiar story just to prove that these things were possible. He motioned with his pipe, 'Another funny thing happened with this same Dan Dowlais and me. We used to knock about together. We were only *crwtyns* of boys, and one Sunday we were playing pitch-and-toss up on the mountain. No harm; just a bit of fun. There were three of us. The third man was called Mog Llewellyn. Mog was a bit of a runner and used to smear himself with oil which made him smell like a horse-stable. But that's by the by. Well, we were in the middle of the game and it was Mog's turn to toss up the three pennies. He spread them on his palm and up they went. Three coins. They made a curve in the air, but only two came down. Two came down! We looked everywhere for the third. We were playing on a grass patch and the grass was as short as the nap on a billiard table, but we combed on our hands and knees over every square inch of it. Then we took off our coats and shook them, and Mog who was getting a bit frantic – superstitious was Mog – said we must take off our trousers, too, and shake them. Well, to humour Mog we took off our trousers, too, though there was only need to look in the turn-ups. But we found nothing. We've never found that penny to this day.' John Davies paused and waved his pipe impressively. 'Three went up and two came down.' He repeated his words like a preacher giving his text. 'Three went up and two came down.'

Uncle Tom went on puffing his pipe for a while, without a crease on his face, then suddenly his moustache began to quiver and he burst out into a high-pitched laughing. He doubled up, and it was some time before he could get his breath back. All the while John Davies was looking at him with bewilderment. At last Uncle Tom spoke. 'Well, John, I've heard a few stories but that one gets the biscuit. Now tell me this...' he had to control himself again before he could carry on, 'tell me this: if old Davey up there was hard up, why didn't he keep the other pennies as well as yours?

It should have been: three went up and none came down, to make it a moral kind of story. A mistake you made in the telling.' He broke again into his high-pitched laughing.

John Davies looked at him dourly, not attempting to conceal his scorn. 'You never would believe in anything, Tom Pritchard, that's your trouble. Always scoffing. Scoff at the Lord and scoff at the chapel.'

Then Uncle Tom chuckled with good humour, 'Now half a mo, John. How can you expect an old backslider like me to believe in miracles, especially when there's a johnny like Dan Dowlais around when they're brewing. Tell me, now?'

John Davies the Blacksmith refused to be drawn any more and, when he took out his tobacco pouch and shared another pipe with Uncle Tom, we knew that they had finished. We got down from the partition with stiff limbs.

As we went into the house Arthur said, 'I thought he was going to talk about explosions. Perhaps we can get him to, later on.' But when we got inside, Dinah had ideas of what we were going to do, and ten minutes later we found ourselves in bed. Yet later, when Nipper had gone to sleep, Arthur came in from the next room and whispered, 'He's down there now, I can hear him. Let's go on the stairs.'

We crept down the back stairs in our nightshirts. We heard Uncle Tom plainly, only he was talking about seed potatoes. It was cold on the stairs and potatoes didn't interest us, so we went back to bed. But on the landing Arthur stood and moving his chin and wiping a big moustache said, 'Aqua fortis, boys. That's the stuff, boys, Aqua fortis,' while Uncle Tom's laugh came piercing its way up from the living-room.

On Thursday afternoon my mother got up from bed for the first time. Dinah had cleaned out the house and was making a special tea to celebrate. The baby was sleeping in the garden as cosy as a nut. The shop was closed on Thursday afternoon and Father had a nap in the middle room, and the whole house was peaceful – not with the strained peace of a Sunday but with the quiet of relief, after the rush and bustle of the previous days.

We were going to have pancakes for tea – Father's favourite dish. Dinah had asked two of us to beat the eggs ready to put into the batter. Afterwards we had taken the bowl of batter outside to stir it. Dinah said the pancakes would be lighter if the batter was stirred outside in the fresh air. Arthur and I had stirred it until our arms ached and we had left the bowl out in the air with a thin muslin cloth over it to keep the dust away. Dinah looked into the bowl and said, 'The pancakes will be so light that they won't come down when I toss them.'

When Dinah mentioned tossing the pancakes, Arthur said that he would like to try tossing them. Dinah said she'd let him, since he wanted to become a chef when he grew up. He'd make a good chef because he was so interested in food. Arthur himself was a bit doubtful about this, and said he would like best to become a traveller with a stock of tins and bottles in a case. Nipper said he would do fine, because he could talk enough already for a whole firm of travellers.

We hurried home from school that afternoon. Mother was already down sitting in the armchair by the fire. It was strange to see her there, since she was always on her feet working, but Father had told her that she had to stay there or go back to bed. So she was sitting in the chair darning socks. The bowl of batter was on the hob and the frying-pan was heating up when we came in. Dinah made the first pancake and Arthur sprinkled the currants in it. Then she showed us the way to toss a pancake, giving the frying-pan a quick forward movement with the wrist. The pancake went up in the air and landed flat in the middle of the pan, lying evenly all round its edge. Arthur put his foot on the fender. 'I'm next. Let me do this one.'

Dinah gave him the pan and poured a small dab of batter into its centre. We all watched him shaking the frying-pan over the fire, impatient for the moment when he would toss the pancake. Dinah gave him a last warning: 'Make sure it's all loose in the pan. Shake it. Here's the knife. There's plenty of fat.'

We all stepped back and held our breath as Arthur stood in the centre of the mat, his feet slightly apart and his tongue in between his teeth. He held the frying-pan in front of him with both hands, and then made one or two movements up and down with the pan as though he was about to throw the pancake. We all shifted impatiently when he stopped.

'Go on. Toss it, Arthur.'

He took up his position again and, after a few more movements, up went the pancake with a shout from Nipper: 'There she goes!' And Arthur caught it as it came down. But it wasn't right in the centre. Although it was done with a beautiful gold on one side, it was spoiled by a white fringe of batter.

'Oh, hard luck! Let me put it right.' With a quick movement of the knife, Dinah slid the pancake back into the centre, but its shape was lost – across the middle was a fold which couldn't be straightened out.

Arthur looked at it doubtfully. 'It's not burned, anyhow.'

Mother said, 'That's fine. Bring it here, Arthur,' and she squeezed a slice of lemon on it. 'I'll have a piece of that one myself when we are ready.'

After the pancakes had been cooked and all was ready, Father came in and said, 'Ah, pancakes! Did I ever tell you about the way they made pancakes in Cefn Colstyn Farm?'

We all said, 'Tell us,' but everyone had a pancake on his plate, and the tea had started before Father told the story.

'Down in Cefn Colstyn they had a big kitchen with a wide old-fashioned fireplace and a big chimney. They made pancakes on a Tuesday right through the year, and the pancakes were known throughout the district for their lightness. If they had a good baking on the farms they'd say, "The bread is as light as Cefn Colstyn's pancakes." They were like snow and nobody knew the secret.'

Father paused and went on with his tea, while Mother tried to hide a smile. Nipper asked, 'What was it? What was the secret? Come on, Pa, tell us.'

'Well, it was simple enough: they gave the pancake plenty of air while it was cooking. When the wife wanted to turn the pancake over, she tossed it up the chimney and then ran outside quick with the frying-pan and caught it before it reached the ground. Then she did the other side and when it was finished it was as light as the air itself.'

Nipper looked at me and then at Father, whose face was

44

still stern. I looked at him and said, 'You didn't tell us how they put the currants in, Pa.'

Father couldn't answer through keeping a straight face, but Arthur said, 'Didn't you know? They shot the currants in with a pellet gun as the pancake was coming down!'

In the middle of the laughing, the door of the scullery opened and someone called out, 'What's going on?'

A small man in a light mackintosh and peak cap, with a brown paper parcel under his arm, came into the room. He looked round and asked, 'Whose birthday?'

'Sit down, Billy. Get Mr Charles a cup of tea, Dinah.'

It was Billy Charles the Yeastman. He came every Thursday, bringing the yeast for the bread and cake baking. He sat in a chair by the fire and, with a tired hand, pushed his cap to the back of his head. His neck was sunk in his shoulders and his eyes were puffed and inflamed. He looked round at us. 'You've got a houseful here and no mistake. You won't half be rich when they all start working.'

He stirred his cup of tea and Dinah offered him a pancake. He shook his head.

'But you must taste the pancakes.'

'No, nothing to eat, on principle.'

My mother looked over at him. 'Go on with you. Taste one of them, Billy. It won't hurt you. Sit over there between two of the lads.'

He put the parcel down but didn't shift from his seat. 'Well, perhaps I will, but I won't sit by the table.'

He never would sit by the table – perhaps afternoon tea was too respectable or too dull for Billy. He took a pancake and tasted it wearily. We were all watching him. He chewed the pancake thoughtfully, then said quite suddenly, 'Very nice indeed,' and, as a thought that seemed to rise out of the very action of his jaws, 'The first bite of anything since yesterday morning.'

'You get worse and worse. The whiskey will be the death of you,' my mother railed him.

He screwed up his face and said persuasively, 'It's not the medicine, Mrs Pritchard. It's my stomach. I've always had trouble with my stomach.'

'I don't believe you have. You don't give it a chance. Have another pancake?'

Billy lifted his hand in the same easygoing gesture I had once seen him give as a greeting to a friend, just before he disappeared into the bar of the Picton.

'You should get married and settle down. Get a woman to look after you. That's the trouble with you, Billy Charles, too long a bachelor!'

He cocked his head as though he were giving this statement great thought. 'Ay, perhaps so.' Then he smiled like a boy, 'If you can find a wife for me who'd make pancakes like these I'd be a converted man.'

He got up and helped himself to another off the plate, and Dinah called across the table, 'Here, pass the plate of pancakes this side, quickly. He's found his appetite.'

Billy Charles was a Thursday afternoon institution. He was always in the same humour; complaining about his stomach, fuddled, taking a joke, telling a story, and selling his yeast as an afterthought.

'I was up in Porth yesterday. Things are pretty slow in the Rhondda. The bottom is dropping out of the Valleys.

They're finished; that's about the truth of it. I used to call on ten shops up there, and now only two of them are open. It will be hitting this valley next, you see if it doesn't.'

Father looked stern and serious, and there was a jarring silence for a few moments until he shrugged his shoulders and said light-heartedly, 'Things will come round again, Billy. It's like the Welsh weather: rain and sunshine; sunshine and rain.'

'Ay, with a bloody sight more rain than sunshine in it, for sure!'

Everyone laughed at Billy Charles' reply and the Thursday afternoon atmosphere came back to the table after the shadow of his bleak prophecy had threatened to spoil the tea party.

He was halfway out of the door after refusing another cup of tea, when Father asked, 'What about the yeast?'

He raised his eyebrows and, without a word, took a penknife out of his pocket and cut a corner off the canvas bag of yeast. Then he walked through into the shop, weighed it, and returned with it wrapped in grease paper. As he left he called out, 'See you next week, and put a couple of pancakes on the hob if I'm late!'

Two of us had to go down to Pontygwaith to tell Uncle Tom that a relation in the Rhondda had died. Father had seen the announcement in the paper that morning, and he was sending it down in case Uncle Tom had missed the paragraph. When any of the clan died, it was a duty to pass on the news of the death even to the most remote members. But Arthur and I, who were to take the message, were glad of the outing, especially since it was Saturday and there was plenty of work to miss. We asked Tom if we could have the horse and trap since I was old enough to drive, but he said, 'Get your boots out. It's only about three miles,'

We set out in the early afternoon to walk down the valley to Pontygwaith. Beyond the village, a big apron of moorland came down to the main road, and it was easy to stray into the bracken looking for a lark's nest or following a scurrying rabbit, but we kept to the road, bored with ourselves and our best suits.

We heard a beer lorry with a trailer rumbling towards us on its way out of the valley, but it was too fast for us to catch and clamber up behind.

We walked on in silence until Arthur mentioned the dead man, Hopkin Llewellyn. Neither of us had ever seen him, but Arthur had all his history: 'He was seventy-four. He was a first cousin to Tom Pritchard and a second cousin to Father. He was in the flooding of the Tynewydd Pit. Haven't you heard the talk about him? Remember that night when Uncle Tom told us how the rescue party got through to the men who were cut off by the water? Hopkin Llewellyn was one of the first to reach them.'

The story came back: 'He carried out the boy who'd been shut in for nine days after the flooding. That was Hop Llewellyn, wasn't it? Didn't he get a decoration?'

'Yes. He and five others went up to London to have it pinned on.'

The dead man was now more alive for us than when he had actually been living. I began to regret that we'd never had a chance to visit him. Now that he was gone, we would never have more than a scanty-lined picture of him. But Uncle Tom, perhaps, would fill it in. Arthur seemed to be thinking the same thing. 'We can ask Tom Pritch to tell us more about him.'

'What did he die from, I wonder.'

Arthur, as serious as ever, answered, 'Old age, no doubt!'

There was nothing more to be said, and we walked along slowly our hands in our pockets, wishing the road wasn't so long, or that we had brought a ball to kick along on our way.

The canal – full of water now – ran parallel to the road for part of the way and we pelted stones into it, making ducks and drakes with the flat ones. Then Arthur discovered a way of having a game and getting nearer to Pontygwaith at the same time. On the side of the road, separating it from the moorland, there was a mound and a ditch which took the water that had drained down from the mountain. The mound was turfed and sloped down to the edge of the road. It was a game to run up the side of the mound at an angle and, keeping a risky footing on its slope, curve down to the road again without putting a foot on the mound's flat top. We swerved along for half a mile enjoying the movement and occasionally coming very near to a spill.

I shouted to Arthur, 'Watch your best trousers, Arthur,' since I was the elder and supposed to be in charge.

Not long after this, I saw him stop at the top of the mound and descend part of the way into the ditch at the other side. As I came up to him he pointed to the neck of a bottle, half hidden in the reeds. I saw the bottle and was puzzled. 'What's up? It's an old empty bottle!'

He said, 'Look at the cork. It's flat with the top of the bottle.'

I caught hold of his hand to steady him, and he reached over and lifted the bottle out of the reeds. It was full of clear brown liquid. There was a label on the bottle but it was dirty and faded by the sun. Arthur said, 'Let's take it with us.'

We held the bottle to the sun. 'Looks like whiskey to me.' I opened my best coat and put the bottle underneath. 'We'll take it to Uncle Tom. He'll know what it is.'

Arthur looked at the bulge in my coat. 'Can't we taste it first? I've got a knife. This will get the cork out. If it's only coloured water we can throw it away.'

Out came the bottle again, and Arthur opened the small blade of his knife and we tried to pierce the cork. A piece came off the top, leaving the liquid still untouched in the bottle.

Just then a farmer came up in an empty gambo. He stopped his horse and looked across at us suspiciously, shouting after a while, 'What you lads got there?'

Arthur was quick with an answer, 'Only a bottle of pop!'

I thrust the bottle back under my coat and we both started walking. I turned round and saw the farmer still watching us. After we'd gone some distance he moved on, shouting something and waving his stick.

Arthur said, 'I wish it were pop. We'd be sure of a drink then.'

Pontygwaith was strung out on both sides of the valley. The pit was on its narrow floor with the canal running alongside. Long streets of houses ran parallel to the valley floor, climbing the hills on both sides like huge flights of stairs, all made of grey stone – as grey as a Sunday. The overhead buckets, taking the slag and the rubbish from the pit, ran straight up this hill over a black cone of coal refuse. On top, the tip itself hung over the valley – a black cloud that had frozen solid to the mountain. They used to say in Pontygwaith, 'It's a place you can roll into easy enough, but it's a different thing to get out.'

God made the world and then he started to make Pontygwaith, but he was tired and handed the work over to the Devil, and it was a Monday morning job for him; even he didn't have his heart in it. You can stand in the valley and put your arms out and touch the mountain on both sides, and if you live here long enough, you'll know what it's like to be dead. But the people in Pontygwaith were the kindliest, liveliest people you'd meet if you circled the earth: they'd sing, box, or sidestep their way through towns ten times the size, and when it came to a strike they stuck it out the longest.

The morning shift was coming up from the pit just as we were going past. We watched the thick stream of men coming from the pithead and hurrying away with their lamps. We stood on the pavement scanning the men's black faces as they passed. All the faces seemed alike. How could we recognise him? Even his moustache would be different; all blackened over with coal dust. The white of the eyes showed up against the black faces, changing the expression and making it hard to recognise even a friend. As we watched, I thought about Jack Morgan who had started

51

work in the pit a week before. He was in the class higher than mine at school. When he went down for the first time, the men told him to sit down and watch, to see how they cut the coal and filled the trams. He told us it seemed years waiting down there, and he asked them a dozen times, 'Is it time to go yet?' At last, at the end of the shift, they said, 'Yes,' and he suddenly remembered that his face was still clean because he'd done no work. He couldn't go home like that! So he got some coal-dust and quickly rubbed it over his face. When he got home he found his father had finished bathing. He asked him, 'How did it go? Let's have a look at you, boy?' When he saw his face, he started to laugh so loud that Jack's mother came in from the back kitchen. Mr Morgan said, 'Look at him, Mam. Look at the finger marks on his face. I did the same myself and that was twenty-three years ago when I started first in the Daran!'

We heard a familiar voice calling out across the road, 'What are you two waiting for? Looking for a start?'

We recognised Uncle Tom. He was smoking a pipe – the one he always hid under a pile of wood on top pit, just before going down. He was not so black as the others. We hurried across the road and straightway started to give the message which we had been carrying like a weight of stones. We both began to speak at once.

'We came to tell you...' Arthur and I exchanged glances and I finished, 'Hopkin Llewellyn died yesterday. It was in the paper.'

He had already started walking on the side path and we fell in beside him. He started his pipe and spat into the gutter, but gave no sign that he had heard the message. Then he said, 'You two boys walked down? You'll be wanting some tea.'

We went up with him to the house in Graig Terrace. It was the last house of the row, with his garden at the back opening onto the mountainside. When he was in his working clothes, Uncle Tom always went in through the back door. He nodded his head and said, 'Come you round with me.'

Aunt Gwen was filling the bath in the back kitchen when we went in. She had grey hair and a pale face but it was flushed with the steam rising from the bath. She had started pouring in the hot water as soon as she heard Uncle Tom's footsteps coming up the pavement. She shook hands and said, 'I wondered who your Uncle had with him. Come by the fire in the kitchen while he's bathing.'

As I sat down in a chair in the living-room, I remembered the bottle. It was still under my coat and I hesitated to bring it out because I knew Aunt Gwen was against anything strong. As she was laying the table, asking us questions about the family and the new baby, she noticed the cautious way I was sitting and at last asked me, 'What have you got under your coat, Willie, a rabbit?'

There was a twinkle in her eye, but when I brought out the bottle her glance was full of suspicion. 'What is it? Have you opened it? Are you sure you found it?' Her quiet voice became shrill and Uncle Tom came in from the other room. He was stripped to the waist and half washed; his front clean and his back still covered with coal-dust – an old Harlequin.

'What's this you're saying about a bottle?' He saw the bottle in my hand and, taking it from me, peered closely at the liquid and then at the label. With one hand he held the bottle and with the other he held up his trousers. 'Where's the cork-screw, Gwennie? Quick!'

His wife scolded, 'You know we haven't got a corkscrew in this house, Tom Pritchard. Finish bathing now so that we can start. These boys are hungry.'

He placed the bottle on the mantelshelf and addressed it. 'Stand you by there, Wass! We'll soon have you open.'

We waited for him to finish and Aunt Gwen left the room to see to the cooking. Arthur had taken a book from a cupboard and was reading, and I looked round at the white hearthstone; the leaded grate, shining like anthracite; the placid china cats on the mantelshelf; and the brass candlesticks, polished every Saturday morning. There was a huge fire in the open grate, and the lumps of coal made the room as hot and as glowing as the mouth of a furnace.

The table was laid with a spotless white cloth. There were four cups on the table: three small ones and a big moustache-cup. Arthur rose from his seat to examine the moustache-cup, when I pointed it out to him. He looked inside and whispered, 'He uses his moustache for a filter!'

Aunt Gwen came in and brewed the tea and called out to Tom. He came in soon afterwards. His face was shining and his moustache bristled out with new vigour. He was in his shirt sleeves and, as he buttoned up his waistcoat, he took out his gold hunter watch and threaded the chain through the buttonhole. He looked thoughtful as he wound his watch slowly; very slowly, until the clicks of the winding dragged wearily one after the other. Just when we thought the spring must surely break, he stopped and, after looking at the face of the watch over his moustache, he snapped the cover to. As he returned the watch to his pocket he said quietly, 'Hop Llewellyn's gone home! It comes to us all, no doubt it comes.' Then he seemed to start back to life and went briskly to the armchair. 'C'mon, boys! Up to the table.'

Aunt Gwen brought in the dishes and the meat. We had forgotten they had their hot meal in the afternoon, and we said we hadn't come to rob them of their dinner. But Uncle Tom said, 'You sit down by there, boyo, and eat what you get on your plate.'

Aunt Gwen smiled and said, 'Plenty here. Eat up and don't be too polite.'

And there was plenty to eat. Tom kept piling the vegetables on our plates and, after the dinner, we had a cup of tea and a biscuit.

While he was drinking his fourth cup, he gave us a merry look and said, 'Well, you haven't done so badly, now. Arthur shall come again, but I'm not so sure about you. You eat too much!'

We got up from the table and Aunt Gwen cleared away the dishes. Uncle Tom went to the mantelpiece for his pipe and saw the bottle. He lit his pipe first, regarding the bottle with a threatening eye. 'We'll soon have him open. Where did you find him?'

We told him and he said, 'Somebody threw him off the back of a beer lorry and meant to come back for him... I hope!'

After searching in a drawer he brought out a thick meat-skewer which he thrust into the damaged cork. He prized it gently till it came out with a faint *plop*. He put the neck of the bottle to his nose and smelled it with caution, and then his face changed gradually from hope to certainty. He called out, 'Where's a glass, Gwennie. Where's a glass?' But his wife didn't come quickly enough and he rummaged in a cupboard until he found an egg cup. He filled the egg cup then he sipped the clear liquid and paused, his moustache moving up and down as he wetted his palate. His face lit up and he half shouted, 'Whiskey, *mun uffern i!*' and back went the egg cup. He filled it up again and said after the second taste, 'And good whiskey at that. What a bit of luck! It's the first bottle of whiskey that's lasted more than a month in this valley, I can say that!' He heard his wife coming in before he could taste it the third time and he re-corked the bottle and put it quickly in the cupboard.

Aunt Gwen came in wiping her hands from the washing up. We all sat round the fire and she took a bagful of socks that wanted repairing. Aunt Gwen never had any children of her own and she always wanted one of our family to go and live with her. It wasn't long before we were being cross-questioned about the new baby: 'What is her name?' And a dozen other questions they ask about new babies.

Uncle Tom was putting on his collar and tie. 'You'll have to let the baby come down here and live with us. You've got enough up there as it is. What do you think about it?'

I shrugged my shoulders, and Arthur said thoughtfully, 'It wouldn't be a bad idea. But you'd have to take her out in the pram on Sunday mornings, Uncle Tom.'

He knotted his tie and looked at Arthur fiercely. 'And don't you think I can manage that? Look here, *bychan*, I pushed one of you – I believe it was your eldest brother – in a go-cart from Ynyswen to Cilhaul; right over the mountain, and then met all the blokes coming off the morning shift on the way back.' He grinned at his wife. 'That was the worst part of the business – they wouldn't leave it rest for weeks.'

Aunt Gwen said, 'Tell me! What colour hair has she, Arthur?'

'I believe she is going to be fair.'

Uncle Tom said, 'That's a change. They've used the tar brush too much on the rest of you.' He turned to his wife and nodded his head. '*Cyw gwaelod y nyth*, Gwen. The chick in the bottom of the nest...'

Arthur finished the proverb: 'Is always a different colour.'

'I hope she is fair then,' I said, half to myself.

Aunt Gwen laughed. 'You'll have to bring her down when she's old enough. Your Uncle can meet you, since he has had so much practice with the pram.'

He nodded his head and said, 'Fine, fine,' but he was ready; dressed to go out. He pulled out his snuff box and offered it to his wife. She put down her darning and took a pinch and held it to her nostrils. We waited for her to sneeze but of course she didn't. She took snuff often, since it was supposed to help her complaint. Before he shut his box he offered it to us, but we both refused since we knew what taking snuff meant. 'Has your Father any of that High Dry left up there now? That was good snuff. It started putting new hair on my head I can tell you. Didn't it, Gwennie?' He pulled his cap off and started smoothing the bald top of his head.

'There's still some High Dry left and there's a new box of Queen's come in.'

'Queen's. Queen's! Well, you are some fine ones. You could have brought a couple of ounces down with you now.'

Aunt Gwen asked quietly, 'Where are you going, Tom?'

He fingered his watch-chain and answered loudly, 'Oh, down the road! Down the road! I'll send these lads a bit of the way and then I'll call up at the Workmen's. There's a Federation meeting tonight, I shan't be late.'

He leaned over and patted her on the shoulder. She very rarely went out and, if anyone were to paint her picture, it wouldn't be right unless she were sitting by the fire, sewing or mending, pale and uncomplaining.

Uncle Tom lit his pipe and we started. As we walked down the street he gave a little history of the people we passed – he knew them all. He took his pipe out of his mouth and held it up in greeting. A huge man with earrings passed and exchanged greetings. 'That's Wil Watkins who played in the forwards for Wales. Best line-out forward for years.'

A bent old man carrying a big parcel under his arm passed on the other side of the street. 'That's Jones the Tailor. He wouldn't give the droppings of his nose away.'

A young woman went by and he raised his cap right off his head. She was dark and showed white teeth as she laughed at his gallantry. 'Ben Williams the Fireman's girl. She'll make a fine wife for somebody.'

The street was like a huge stone channel; the houses were all of rough-faced stone, and the pavements of huge flag-stones were flush with the walls of the houses. Up here the pavements and the walls were clean – the dust from the colliery never rose as high, and when it rained the water, rushing down in a small spate, washed clean the gutters. Many of the front doors of the houses were open. Uncle Tom stopped at one and, leaning over the step, shouted up the passage, 'Mrs Mordecai, is Dai home yet?'

A woman's voice answered shortly from the back of the house. 'No, not yet. Is that you, Mr Pritchard? Come on in.'

'No, no. You won't get me out if I come in. Tell your Dai when he comes in that we got the seven pounds of shallots and he can have half when he likes.'

We followed him down the street until we came to the Workmen's Hall – a huge building like a stone box faced with red bricks. There was a group of men standing outside. A man shouted out, 'Are you coming up later, Tom?'

Uncle Tom nodded and raised his pipe. A man detached himself from the second group and came over to us. He was a square man with no flesh on his face and his trousers had wide bottoms and no turn-ups like a sailor's. He said, 'You'll see about that sick pay, Tom.'

'Don't you worry, Huwcyn. That'll be all right.'

Huwcyn looked at us without smiling. 'Who are these, Tom?'

'Nephews from up the valley. Do you like the look of them?'

The other grinned in a friendly way. Uncle Tom said, 'I'm just going to the bottom of the road and I'll see you here after the meeting. You leave it to me.'

Huwcyn nodded his head and then he gave Tom a knowing look and asked, 'What about the widow tonight, Tom?'

Uncle Tom looked at us and then he turned to Huwcyn and pulled his pipe out, using it to tap him on the shoulder. He said in Welsh, 'Look here, Huwcyn Morgan. When you talk that way your mouth is as big as the up-cast in the pit down there. What's more, man, there's nothing in it but bad air neither.'

Huwcyn looked at Uncle Tom whose face was quite straight. He grinned and said, 'All right, Tom. I'll only use it to eat my supper. No offence.'

Uncle Tom rose his pipe and, as we walked away, he said, 'See you later.'

We left him halfway down the street. He put his hand in his pocket and gave us sixpence each. He said, 'Don't get drunk now, and don't forget the way down here another time soon.'

As we were going Arthur asked, 'What are you going to do with the bottle of whiskey?'

The answer came back straight. 'Oh, I'm going to keep it to rub in my back when I get the sciatica.'

After being with Uncle Tom you had a better feeling than if you'd been to the pictures and, in the end, he wasn't the sort of chap to say, 'And don't forget to go straight home.'

When we got to the bottom of the road, we turned and we could still see him walking up the middle of the road, his pipe in his hand and his elbow raised in greeting at every few yards.

PART II

It was getting dark as we walked up from Pontygwaith. The air was warm and perfectly still. Arthur said, 'What a beautiful night it will be. You could sleep out tonight. The ferns would keep you warm.'

'Yes, till about two o'clock in the morning. It gets as cold as ice then.'

'How do you know?' Arthur asked quickly, 'Have you ever been out at that time?'

I nodded my head. I was proud to boast that I had seen the Great Bear balancing on the tip of his tail, but I was loathe to remember the occasion.

It was like Arthur not to take a nod for an answer; he persisted. 'When? During the war? Or was it the time the cow calved?'

'No. I had to go to bed then, before it happened. John

61

Davies the Blacksmith, who was there, said, "No need for the *crwtyn* to stay." And I was so tired I was glad to go.'

Arthur was still waiting; he was like a dog that had found a scent – nothing would lead him off.

I said, 'The fern is pretty tough to cut now, when it's green. You'd have to pluck it up by the roots to make a bed. It cuts your, hands, too.'

Arthur paid no attention. 'You said it was very cold. What time of the year was it?'

At last I made up my mind to tell him the whole story – he wouldn't rest until he knew it all. 'It was June last year. Perhaps you can remember – they said there was a nightingale in that willow-bed alongside the canal, not far from the colliery.'

'Did you and Tom go to hear it?' He'd found the real scent. He considered for a while, then he said thoughtfully, 'I remember quite well. You were in bed the next day. Didn't you have a cold or something? There was a joke between you and our Tom, about the nightingale. What happened? Tell me.' He stopped suddenly, then he looked at me and his face lit up. He shouted, 'I've got it. No! Don't tell me. You fell into the canal!' He saw my face and knew he was right; he started to laugh, sitting down on the bank at the side.

I could see the fun of it now, after all that time, and I sat down on the bank, too, and told him, 'There was talk of the nightingale all over the town, so our Tom said, "We'll go. This is no hoax. They say Ebenezer the Preacher has heard it. You put two waistcoats and a scarf on, and we'll go down about eleven o'clock tonight." So a long time after you'd all gone to bed we had some cocoa and walked down the canal bank. The nightingale was supposed to start about eleven-thirty, just when the moon was coming up over Mynydd Leyshon...'

Arthur interrupted, very seriously. 'It isn't likely that there could have been a nightingale. I read in a book that Lloyd George said, "There are no nightingales this side of the Severn."'

I was annoyed at his spoiling the atmosphere for the story. 'To blazes with Lloyd George! What does he know about nightingales?'

'Did you hear it then?'

But now that I was telling the story, I wasn't going to be rushed to the end of it. 'There was a crowd of people there when we got down. They were lying on the canal bank and standing about in groups. There were girls down there, too, and there was a lot of giggling and shouting enough to frighten any nightingale away, until someone – I believe it was Jack Ragtime – shouted for quiet. But we didn't hear a thing, though we spoke in whispers for half an hour. Then they started singing. It was the finest singing I've heard outside the choirs. The air was soft and they weren't singing too loudly like the crowds do sometimes, but they were keeping it low, and in time, perfectly. The moon made the canal look clean, and if you half closed your eyes you could almost think you were by the sea.'

'Almost,' said Arthur. 'It's more like a sewer, down there.'

'They sang for an hour and everybody was sitting or lying down on the grass at the edge of the canal by this time. But there was no nightingale. I just listened to the singing, but when they started again, the voices seemed to go further and further away. I was lying down right at the edge of the canal and, although it was cold, there was such a crowd that, tucked in the middle of it, I was warm enough to doze. Anyhow, I went right off to sleep, and thinking I was in bed I must have tumbled over, because the next thing I knew I was in the canal and everybody shouting and our Tom lying on his stomach on the bank holding my collar and saying, "It's all right. I've got him." Then they pulled me out and Tom made me run every yard of the way home with him. He gave me something strong that burned its way down my throat, and then I went to bed, and they made me stay there until the following afternoon.'

After some time Arthur asked, 'Did anyone hear the nightingale?'

'Well, they said they heard him after we'd gone home.'

'I don't believe there was a nightingale there. Even if there was, it wouldn't have sung. A sparrow wouldn't sing in a place like that.'

I didn't try to discuss with him whether a sparrow does sing or not, or try any further to convince him that there had been a nightingale. Besides, I wasn't sure myself. Less so now, as I thought about it again and asked myself: how was it possible for a bird with such a fine sense to live by water that must have smelled like my clothes did after I'd been hauled out of it?

As we drew near home, a remark of Arthur's kept running in my mind: 'You could sleep out tonight'. Sleep out! That's a thing we'd never done. Whenever we had made a tent, we had always to pull it down before dark.

Perhaps in the holidays we could persuade them at home to let us camp up on the mountain, even if it were only for one night.

I said nothing to Arthur, but the thought kept warm a corner of my mind until the breaking up of school for the summer holidays. Then, in the long days between jobs in the warehouses and in the shop, I cast round for material for a tent: first of all a piece of old sail-cloth which had been used to cover the cart in wet weather; a big canvas wrapper; and a two-hundredweight maize sack which we cut and opened out. The scheme got too big for me to hold myself, so I told Arthur and Nipper and they helped me to find the poles. Bit by bit we gathered the things together for the camp: a collier's lamp from Uncle Tom; a horserug, a bit moth-eaten but still very warm; a groundsheet; and a pound of candles. Then there was nothing to do but to wait for the hazy, warm spell that comes in August after the rain, when every morning the top of Gilfach-y-Rhydd mountain shows up as clean as the forehead of a young girl. Father gave us his permission – we asked him on a Thursday afternoon – and everything was ready in the house.

We had to decide who was to go, but that was easy enough. The tent was big enough for five: there were Arthur, Nipper, and myself, and Fatty Hughes – his father would let him sleep out; he was funny, too – and lastly Ginger Williams, who would come whether his father was willing or not. After this was settled, the next thing was to find a place to pitch the tent. Ginger Williams, Fatty and I went up Mynydd Leyshon one afternoon to look for a likely spot.

Going up the hill Ginger said, 'It must be near water. You always have a camp near water.'

We all agreed on that, but where was there a spring on the top of the mountain? There were many halfway down, but it was understood – although we'd not talked about it – that we would camp nowhere else but on top.

We reached the flat top of the hill and slanted round a sheep-wall which encircled a big meadow. Near the centre of the meadow and in a hollow was a copse of trees and a small stream running away from it. After looking round, we climbed the wall and crossed over to the trees – they were lithe, silver birch – and followed the stream to its source: a big moss-covered rock where it issued as a spring.

Ginger Williams got down on his knees and, cupping his hands, took a mouthful of water. 'Lovely,' he said, 'only it's cold enough to freeze your old granny.'

'That's all right, Ginge,' Fatty Hughes said, 'we're not bringing her with us. But this is the place for us. Look, there's a flat bit of turf over there.' He pointed to a small clearing, and we all agreed that it was the place.

The next thing was to get permission. 'This field belongs to old Pugh, Y Garth Fawr. You know him – he brings a gambo of turnips down every year to sell round the houses.'

Ginger said, 'Let's go up the farm and ask him. I remember my old woman bought some from him, he doesn't seem a bad sort of bloke.'

Fatty Hughes, who found it hard climbing walls, pointed to the end of the field. 'There's a gate up there. That leads to the farm, no doubt.'

The three of us crossed the field to the gate with more

boldness than we had in entering, but when we got to the lane which led from the gate, we were strolling with less purpose.

'Who's going to do the talking?' Fatty asked nervously.

'I will,' Ginger said readily, 'but...' and his voice tailed off a little, 'we can all put a word in, like.'

'That's the best idea. The three of us can say enough to keep going.'

But we came on Pugh the Garth unexpectedly; we met him on a turn in the lane just before coming to the farm yard, and we didn't have a sentence between us. The old feud between the farmers and the boys from the valley was between us like a wall. He looked at us shrewdly and, seeing there was no harm in us, said in a high sing-song, 'And what would you boys be wanting this afternoon? Come up for some eggs you have?'

We shook our heads.

'Come up to give me a hand with the milking then?' He looked at us with a twinkle in his eye and, grinning with relief, we all started talking at once, so that there was only a mixed-up jumble of words.

The farmer interrupted, 'Half a minute now. I never heard three magpies go at it so well. One at a time. You have a go first.' He pointed at Fatty with his stick.

Fatty gulped and then came out with, 'We were looking for a place to camp, Mr Pugh. And we were thinking that there'd be a place on your farm where we could put up a tent.'

I made up my mind to pat Fatty on the back for that little speech, but Mr Pugh the Farmer didn't think it was a good speech, it seemed. His eyes weren't twinkling any more, they were farmer's eyes after someone had mentioned his property – hard and cautious.

'A place to camp on my farm, eh?' He put down his stick hard. 'I've never had campers on my farm, and I'm not going to start now.'

'We've only got a small tent,' I said hopefully.

And Ginger, not to be behind, added, 'There's a lovely place with water down in those birch trees in the big meadow.'

Mr Pugh stiffened up, and his voice went to its highest pitch. 'Camp in the big meadow!' Then he started to laugh loudly and we knew that we had made a wrong step. 'Let campers in my big meadow! You may as well come and camp in the parlour in my house. No, not until they grow pomegranates in Penstephan! No, not if you paid me five pounds a week in ground rent.'

We were silent, not knowing quite what was our next move.

Ginger said tamely, 'Well, we were only asking, Mr Pugh.'

He raised his stick and looked at us more benevolently. 'Yes, yes, yes! No harm, no harm! But I'll tell you what: you boys don't want to camp in no fields. Look, there's the whole of the mountain, and good springy turf to put your tent on. Then, there's a place, ay, there's a place.' He stumped his stick hard on the ground. 'The very spot. I'll tell you where. Go down to the sheep-wall and follow it right along until you come to the cattle-pound. You can camp there, and welcome. And you can come up to the well in the farmyard for water.'

We thanked him but he was already moving off round

the corner of the lane, waving his stick to us as he disappeared.

Before we started we had a conference. Ginger asked, 'What's a cattle-pound?'

'Never heard of it.'

None of us knew. Then we agreed that it would be better to follow the wall and perhaps we would stumble across it, whatever it was.

We reached the end of the lane and skirted the wall, wading through the sharp-smelling fern which grew right up to its foot.

After we'd gone for about half a mile without coming across anything that looked like this strange thing, a cattle-pound, Ginger stopped and, turning round on the narrow track through the fern, said thoughtfully, 'Do you think old Pugh was having a game with us? Pulling our legs, like. Cattle-pound! What does it mean? It sounds a bit like fetching pigeon's milk to me.'

We stopped, and Ginger and I climbed the wall to look round. There was a field of oats at the other side of the wall, stretching away in front of us, and on the further side there was a dark fringe topping the green line of the crop, as if the wall curved back around the oat field.

'I believe I can see the end of this wall. Let's go on. I don't think he was pulling our legs. But even if we don't find the cattle-pound, there may be a clearing in the bracken where we can put our tent.'

We strung out and started again, and after we had walked for another quarter of a mile the wall swung sharply to the right, and just beyond the bend there was a break in it, closed by a two-barred gate. We ran to the gate and looked over. We saw an enclosure about the size of a kitchen garden; triangular in shape with its diagonal formed by a length of wall that cut off the corner of the oat field. The small area was floored by close-clipped turf, as green and as even as a bowling-green. We jumped over and felt the soft turf under our feet.

Fatty called out, 'Oh, this is the place, boys! Come into the parlour!'

Ginger said, 'This must be it. They could keep cattle in here, no doubt.'

'There haven't been any cattle here for years,' said Fatty.

The turf was unspoiled except for a large flat stone, dislodged from the top of the wall.

'What a grand place! You could feel safe in here. Nobody could see the tent and come bothering.'

Ginger said, 'We'll have it in the corner there. We'll only want two upright poles, then – we can use the angle of the wall for the other supports. Look at this stone: it's as clean as if an old woman had been up here scrubbing. You could eat your dinner off it.'

'This will be better than a holiday at the seaside.'

'What about the water? It's a long way back to the farm.' Fatty groaned and sat down on the stone.

'You would!'

'But there ought to be a short cut to the farm from here.'

We climbed onto the wall and soon spotted a path starting higher up, where a hedge joined the wall. It cut straight across the fields to the farm.

Everything was now clear for the adventure. We decided

that we should start in the morning. The weather was good and it was better to start before anything turned up. As Ginger said, 'The sooner the better. Our whippet may go off his feed, then I'll have to be there to keep running down to the chemist's.'

There was a path running through the bracken, straight towards the shoulder of the hill. Before going down to the valley, we stopped and sat on a flat boulder by the side of the path.

The valley below was bright in the sun. Except for a fine haze of dust, hanging like a black beehive over the pit, everything was different. The sun had made luminous the grey stone of the houses, and softened the ugly bulk of the tiny streets, cemented onto the hillsides. They were playing cricket on the Welfare Ground below. The batsman made his stroke and the soft *plomp* of the ball hitting the bat came up a second afterwards.

Fatty drew his knees under his chin and pointed to the village. 'Not a bad place. I'd sooner live here as anywhere.'

Ginger nodded his head and then he said slowly, 'If ever I go to Cardiff I want to get back before the end of the day. You feel nice and cosy in the valley. I wouldn't have been born anywhere else.'

'Me, too!'

The prospect of camping out cast as peaceful a light as the sun. We went home glowing with plans, and arranging to meet early in the morning.

I woke very early, hearing the clump of boots on the pavement – the first shift going to work – and Arthur and I got up and were downstairs just as the six-thirty hooter was going for stop-bond. About an hour later we heard Ginger and Fatty calling from the canal bank at the back. They had their kit tied in a big bundle, and Ginger had a sack with coal, as well. We lowered the tent and our own bundles into the dry bed of the canal and, before we started, I ran into the house to see Dinah: I wanted to make sure that she would send Nipper up later with the food, as we had arranged. She was feeding the baby out of a small dish, and she was giving her all her attention.

After waiting for a while I asked her what was in the dish. She looked up smiling, 'You'd better take some with you. It's quite easy to make, and quite nice really.'

I screwed up my nose. Dinah had been joking about the camp all along. She told Mother when we asked her about staying out. 'Let them go, Ma. One night on the mountain will cure them. They'll soon be back to their feather beds!'

Although she'd done everything to help us to get away, she still kept ragging us. This morning she asked, 'How long are you going to stay up there?'

'It all depends,' I said evasively.

'On whether you can stick it or not, you mean?'

'Oh, we'll stick it,' I said jauntily, 'if the weather holds out. We can't stay in the rain, because we're not sure if the tent will keep water out.'

'That's lucky,' she said as she turned the baby over onto her front and started stroking her back. 'She's got the wind.'

I bent down and saw the baby's face getting red and distressed. She was choking or something. I said to Dinah quickly, 'You'd better put her right side up. Quick, she's suffocating!'

Dinah looked at me with wide eyes and I coolly examined the baby. Then she said, 'Well! So his lordship has deigned to notice the baby.'

I was angry. 'Come on, stop fooling now. Will you send Nipper up with some food, about ten o'clock?'

Ignoring my question, she lifted up the baby and faced her towards me. 'There, have a look at one of your brothers. A good look – you don't see him often.'

I stamped about impatiently. 'Come on now. My pals are out there waiting for me.'

She asked, 'Who's going to cook?'

It was no use trying to hurry her – she had the whip hand, so I said with a confidence I didn't feel, 'Oh, I'm going to cook!'

She gave the baby a knowing smile, which was more irritating than if she had said outright, 'And what cooking it will be!' At last, when she had made me watch the baby's antics whilst she was being fed, she said, 'All right, I'll pack the food and I'll send David up with it, as soon as we've finished breakfast.'

I got ready to make my escape, but for a moment I hesitated, not knowing whether to say goodbye as if we were going on a real holiday, or pretend that we were coming back that afternoon. After putting on my cap I said casually, 'Well, so long,' and went out.

Laughing, she called me back. 'Aren't you going to kiss the baby?' But I was already over the canal wall.

We tied the bundles to the poles and Ginger and I, who were about the same size, took one pole with the suspended bundles, while Fatty and Arthur took the other.

We met no one on our way out of the village and we were glad, because if the expedition was a failure and we had to come back, there would be fewer people who knew about it.

We got the stuff up the hill without difficulty, and set to work straightway to put up the tent, and to make a stone fireplace for the cooking. Then we went outside the pound and gathered armfuls of fern to strew on the floor of the tent. With the fern we also stuffed up the chinks in the corner of the wall. We stretched the sail-cloth over the top and weighted it down onto the wall with stones. With the horse-cloth we made a flap for the tent and, when we had carried the flat stone and placed it in the centre for a table, most of our building was done.

Ginger made the fire, while Fatty and I went for water. We found our way to the farm easily enough, and by the time we returned Nipper had brought the food up in a big frail with mugs and plates and a bottle. We set to work and cooked a meal: fried bacon and potatoes.

After clearing away we sat down to decide what we were to do with the rest of the day, the greater part of which was still unspent.

Arthur said, 'Let's go looking for Roman remains. We can follow the Roman road and look around. There's supposed to be plenty on this mountain.'

But Ginger shook his head. 'Roman remains! I don't like the sound of that. Not for the first day at any rate. What about a game of football?'

'Too hot.'

'What about some fishing?' Fatty asked, 'I've got a line

– I packed it in with my stuff.'

We praised Fatty's foresight and agreed that it should be fishing.

'But where are the fish?' asked Arthur.

'In the reservoir.'

'But you have to have a permit to fish there.'

'How much?'

'One and sixpence. You get it from Mynachdy Farm, across the Cwm.'

This made us consider: it was a lot of money to pay for an uncertain number of fish. Besides, it was doubtful whether we could raise such a sum, and it looked as if fishing was off. Then Ginger got up and said decisively, 'We don't want a permit, we can chance it. There's enough of us to keep watch. C'mon.'

We set out for the reservoir with much more zest than we would have done had we bought a permit. We took the short cut across the field and, when we were well past the Garth Farm, we cut a tall hazel stripling out of a hedge and trimmed it into a rod, and while we were doing this Fatty and Nipper scouted for worms.

The reservoir lay across a narrow glen that hung from the side of the central block of hills. A small stream had been dammed and around the sheet of water they had planted a fringe of young birches. The whole was enclosed by a high wall. It was miles from any village, and the nearest farmhouse was out of sight, around a spur of the hill. It was a little park set in the midst of a barren, heather-strewn moorland.

When we reached the foot of the wall, it looked at first

glance as if it were impossible to climb. But there was no glass on top and, after Ginger had hauled himself up, standing on my shoulders, he hoisted each of us up in turn. We crouched down at the other side of the wall and Ginger took charge as we made plans.

'All stay here, while Willie and I go to see if there's anyone inside.'

Ginger and I threaded our way carefully through the small birch trees which were hardly higher than our shoulders. The water was without a ripple, like a sheet of grey-blue glass. A few birds were paddling on the fringe of water at the far side.

'Moorhens, I believe. They're pretty shy, so there's not likely to be anyone here.'

We whistled to the others and, as they came up, Ginger gave the orders: Fatty to guard first without showing his head above the wall – there was a bank inside where he could stand; and then Nipper and Arthur to take a turn together. The rest of us went to a spot which looked a likely place to fish from, and I hooked a worm and hopefully threw the line. The others sat down on the bank, quite ready to be impressed even by the smallest of fishes.

But nothing happened. We watched the line for a long time in silence, until Arthur and Nipper got restless. We motioned them away and they strolled off upstream.

Ginger came and sat nearer to me and whispered, 'Are you sure about the fish?'

'There's trout here. Dai Jeremiah's father comes up regular, and he catches some.'

Ginger's silence after this seemed to show some doubt.

'Keep the rod lower.'

I lowered it but there was no change, the line hung loose and dispirited. Then I handed it over. He lifted the line out of the water and examined the bait.

'He's still there but they seem to have had a bite at him. We'll change him, perhaps he's toughish.'

We watched patiently for another half hour, but still no result. Then the two others came back.

Arthur grinned. 'How many have you got?' Ginger motioned with his hand but Arthur went on, 'You won't catch anything. You want a fly not a worm. You can't catch trout with a worm.'

Just then we heard a whistling and I said, 'It's Fatty, we've forgotten all about him.'

When Arthur and Nipper had gone, Ginger said, 'I think he's right.' Then he said loudly in his natural voice, 'There's more in this fishing than you'd think.'

Fatty came up and we were glad to hand the rod to him. As he looked hopefully at the float we asked, 'See anything?'

'Nothing on legs. There's a sparrow-hawk just outside the wall. He's got his eye on something and keeps hanging on the air like a feather.'

We went over to see the hawk but the other two said they had seen it glide down the wind without making its swoop. We left them and walked on to the deep end of the reservoir, where there was a wooden pier running out to a small tower, built like a castle. We walked on to the pier and Ginger, thinking he saw a fish, signalled to Fatty to bring the rod across. After watching Fatty dangling the rod over the iron rail – still without result – we turned to the tower. When Arthur and Nipper saw us on the pier they came across too, and the watch was forgotten.

The tower was made of rough stone and the thick door, painted brick-red, was in strange contrast to the rest of the building. We tried the door and found it was open, and we all crowded in. After our eyes had got used to the darkness we saw three control wheels mounted on columns, like the driving wheel of a tram-car.

Fatty said, 'What a place! Haunted I expect.' He was always smelling out ghosts.

Ginger inspected the wheels, and Arthur and I peered through the chinks in the wooden floor. Ginger, who was turning one of the wheels, said, 'I wonder what they are for? To control the water level, I expect.'

'Now's your chance, Ginger,' said Fatty. 'You let all the water out, and we'll gather the fishes!'

Ginger looked up from the wheel quickly, and a wild light came into his eyes, but he shook his head, rejecting the idea after a moment's thought. 'We'd get some fish but there'd be too much water.'

Arthur, seeing the fishing-rod lying idle, went out to try his luck, saying as he went, 'If you're going to mess about there, someone had better guard.'

But Ginger had been stirred by Fatty's suggestion of controlling the water. He turned to me. 'I wonder what will happen if we do turn a couple of them. C'mon, we'll see what will happen. Go outside, Fatty, and take Nipper and see if any more water flows out when we turn. You take that wheel, Willie.'

Fatty, though a bit alarmed, did as Ginger suggested, saying before he went to the wall, 'Don't turn too much – they'll know down in the village if there's a lot of water in the stream. No! No! Don't turn till I get there.'

Ginger and I started turning the wheels slowly, watching Fatty through the open door. His back was towards us as he looked over the parapet at the stream below. Nipper was standing beside him. We turned the wheels for some time without Fatty giving a sign that he had seen an increase in the flow of water. So we stopped and shouted to him, 'Seen anything?' He shook his head and we went back to the turning, working much faster until the effort made us sweat.

At first Fatty still kept looking down, immovable against the parapet, then suddenly he shot up and started dancing about, waving his arms and shouting frantically, 'Stop! stop!' He looked over the parapet and still continued to shout, running backwards and forward on top of the wall. Ginger and I began to reverse the wheels. I turned and took a glance at Ginger's face to see if he was scared, but it was only screwed up with the effort of pulling the wheel round.

Fatty came running up the pier, shouting, 'Oh, stop it. Can't you? Stop it!' and Ginger and I turned with all our strength. But Nipper, who had stayed beside the wall all the time, presently signalled that the flow of water had gone back to normal. We gave a few more turns to the wheels and then sat down against the wall of the tower, wiping our faces.

Ginger grinned at me and pointing at the wheels said, 'They must work it.'

Nipper came in and I asked him, 'Was it much, Nip?'

'No,' he said coolly, 'I've seen more water in the gutter. You ought to have kept on.'

Fatty came up after being out again to inspect the stream. 'Not much! It was like a small Niagara. You must have let out a couple of thousand gallons!'

Ginger said, 'Plenty more there, anyway.'

But Fatty was beginning to get nervous and kept worrying us to leave the reservoir quickly before someone came up. But a shout from Arthur caused another delay. He had been fishing all the time unmoved by the commotion.

'He's caught something,' Nipper shouted.

We ran out and saw him taking a very small fish off the hook. Ginger slapped him on the back. 'Good boy, Arthur. We must have stirred them up by letting the water out.'

Arthur looked at the fish. 'You didn't stir the big 'uns up though, I think he's a minnow!'

Fatty interrupted, 'Come on, Arthur. We got to go. There may be some more fish further down the stream.'

As we were walking off the pier, Nipper pointed down at the watermark below. 'It's not gone down half an inch,' he said disgustedly.

We dropped down over the wall and cut straight across the moorland. When we were a safe distance away we sat down out of sight in the fern. 'We can leave the rod here,' Ginger said, 'unless anyone wants to do some more fishing.'

No one was eager, not even Arthur. 'Break it up, and if anybody meets us we've just been studying nature.'

'Let's have another look at the fish, Arthur.'

Arthur put his hand into his pocket and took out the

fish. He held it in the palm of his hand, and it looked a
sorry thing.

'Wait a minute,' Fatty said as he cut two fern leaves. He
placed them underneath the fish. 'It looks much bigger
now, but thank goodness we never got a permit.'

We returned by a different way: instead of following the
stream we climbed onto higher ground, to a flat-topped
ridge strewn with large boulders. 'Giant stones,' Fatty
called them, and the tableland did look as if two giants had
run amok, pelting each other with boulders, scattering
them widespread and denting the earth where they fell.
They were of all shapes and stood at all angles, and five of
us could hide easily behind the biggest. There was one
unusual-looking stone – it lay a little way off from the
confusion of the other stones. It was almost a perfect
oblong and was so flat and smooth that it looked as if it
had been cut. It was about eight feet long, and lay in short-
napped turf. Attracted by the regular appearance of the
stone, we examined it very carefully. I liked the look of it –
it was so different from the others.

'Perhaps it's an old Druid stone. It's a bit like the shape.'

Arthur was doubtful. 'There's always a lot of those
together. Maybe it's a burial stone!'

Fatty expanded, 'Perhaps there's a cave underneath and
something hidden there!'

All these imaginings warmed the blood: I saw the golden
necklace of a Celtic maiden carved beautifully in the form
of a serpent; a vase of Roman coins, or a sword inlaid with
precious stones.

Ginger got up and started circling the stone. 'Do you

think there's anything valuable underneath?'

Fatty, carried away, said, 'Some ducats perhaps. Let's have a look!'

We were all ready to lift the stone and we soon had our fingers underneath one side of it. At first we didn't move it an inch but, after resting and spreading ourselves out in better positions, we tried again. This time we lifted it a few inches off the ground but, after holding it and getting no further, we had to let it drop. We sat down upon it and admitted that we were beaten, though not very disappointed, because whatever we had found, it would never have been as bright and shining as the things we had imagined.

Fatty bent down and spoke into a small chink underneath the stone, 'It's all right, boss. You can rest another thousand years. We'll call you when we've got the garden straight.'

We were getting hungry so we pushed on towards the camp, passing here and there big heaps of light-coloured pebbles as big as skulls, which the farmers had gathered ready for carting. Further on, we struck the old Roman road and then we soon reached the camping site. Everything was as we left it, and immediately we set about making a fire to cook the meal.

At dusk we carried the embers of the fire and placed them in the centre of the tent space, where they lit up the tent with a rich glow. We were eager to get inside the tent; to sit in a house we had built ourselves, around a hearth of our own making. It was the first time any of us had slept out and, more exhilarating than this, it was the first time we had broken away from the family and escaped a protection that was sometimes too complete. As we hugged the bright cosiness of the tent – now a real house, since the fall of darkness – we felt: this is an adventure; this is what it is to live.

Outside, stars were appearing in a blue velvet sky and, just beyond the opening of the pound, a glow-worm was shining from a small clump of bracken, like the reflection of a bright star in a pool. We tried to find it, using the lamp, but it was as difficult as seeing a candle beam at noon. We took the lamp and hung it to a cross-pole of the tent.

Ginger showed us how to trim the wick from the bottom of the lamp, just as the collier does. He said, 'My father uses one of these lamps. They're better than the bobby-dazzler electric ones. They don't make your eyes ache, and you can tell straightway if there's gas.'

Fatty said, 'My father uses one of those too. He's on the afternoon shift. He's coming up about this time.'

Ginger asked, 'What district does he work?'

'Down in Ianto Pendar's. His working place is right underneath that plantation on the other side of the valley.'

'My father works right underneath this mountain. When he goes in, he's got to walk two and a half miles from the pit bottom out in this direction. Perhaps his place is right underneath here! But he's not down there now. He's on the morning shift.'

Fatty grinned. 'He may wake us up in the morning, Ginge, when he starts clouting the face.'

'If he knew we were on top he'd give an extra large thump to that coal, for sure he would.'

Arthur asked, 'How far down is it?'

'Just short of half a mile.'

'He'd have to slam the coal pretty hard to wake us up, then.'

'Ay, he would,' Ginger admitted, 'but he's a good collier, fair play. During the war, when they wanted men to go to France to dig tunnels and dug-outs in the Front, they sent for my old toff, with Wil Jones Slogger, and a bloke from Pont-shon-Norton – the three best colliers in the pit. He was out there for nearly three years, though he said once if he could swim he'd have been home much sooner. He won't tell us much about it.'

We heard footsteps outside the pound and the talking stopped abruptly. Fatty Hughes jumped up but Ginger motioned him to sit down and keep quiet. After a breathless half-minute a voice called out, 'Who's in there?'

Ginger stood up, clenching his fists, and shouted back in a harsh voice, 'What do you want?'

There was no answer, and Ginger and I took pieces of stone from out of the wall – we felt much braver with the stones clasped tightly in the hand. We looked at one another, wondering what to do, but then the voice called back, 'Oh, it's all right,' and the figure of a man appeared dimly in the opening of the wall. 'I saw your light and I came across to kindle my pipe.'

The voice was pleasant and we were reassured. The man climbed over the gate and we waited for him to come into the light. I was relieved when I recognised him as a man from New Street. I'd seen him about a lot recently – he'd injured his foot in the colliery and limped about with a stick. He was a quiet-spoken man and, as he lit his pipe and chatted, our fear melted away. He stood in front of the tent and asked us our names and where we came from. He said he knew Fatty's father, and that he had been out of the pit, because of his accident, for nearly six months. He then went on to say he'd been doing other work; furthering 'the cause'. A picture of him preaching in one of the streets suddenly came back to me. And, standing there with the fire lighting up his face and showing the hollows of his cheeks, he asked us whether we had been 'saved'. He caused as much a stir by this question as when he had first shouted. I shifted uneasily and didn't know what to answer; Ginger poked the fire doggedly as if he hadn't heard the question; Fatty continued to stare at the man as he had done since he came in.

But he didn't wait for an answer; he went on, 'Praise the Lord, I am saved. And when the Trumpet sounds, I shall be taken up wherever I am. If I'm in the pit working, at the first blast of the Trumpet my tools will drop out of my hands and I shall be taken up right through the earth from the very spot, as white as a lily, with all uncleanness washed away.' He said all this in a quiet, even voice as though he were talking about the most everyday thing, and when he left as suddenly as he came, wishing us good night, we were too amazed to reply.

Wonder at his strange words was followed by uneasiness. Fatty asked quickly, 'Do you believe what he says?'

Arthur, who had been looking at the man levelly without saying anything the whole time, said firmly, 'I do not. It's impossible; it would have to be a miracle!'

85

'You are right,' said Ginger. 'And it would be a miracle if he came out of the Daran pit as white as a lily!'

We laughed and soon forgot about the incident after Ginger's remark, and since Nipper was already asleep we made our beds and turned in.

We slept until the early hours of the morning when we were wakened by Fatty, who sat up and said sharply, 'What's that? What's that?' He said he had heard horses' hoofs distinctly.

We listened but we could hear nothing and, grumbling, went back to sleep.

We slept fitfully on the hard bed and woke up soon after dawn, unrested and a little dispirited. The pound was grey and ugly; there was a heavy mist and the air was cold. The sticks were damp and we couldn't get the fire started for nearly an hour. Fatty started to sneeze and began to search around for a reason why he must go home. The camp was beginning to totter, but then the sun came up benevolently, and by the time we had eaten breakfast only the previous day was remembered; the night was forgotten.

We played football until it got too hot, and then we sat down on a bank of heather and discussed what we we're going to do. Arthur suggested walking over to Pentre where the big explosion had taken place, but Fatty said, 'It's too far, count me out. It's miles and miles!'

'But you can stay behind and guard the tent.'

He considered and after a while said, 'All right, Nipper and I will stay. We can make some chips, Nipper.'

As the rest of us set out, I remembered the Sunday afternoon after the explosion: over four hundred men were killed and people came from the other valleys and passed through our village as they walked over to Pentre. All were in their Sunday clothes, and they made a slow moving line that circled the mountain like a mourning band. That happened six years before, though the war had made people forget the explosion.

We walked through narrow lanes with high-hedged pastures on each side, and then across a big common. We stopped here to gather whinberries. Further on, passing a ruined farmhouse, we came to the brink of a hollow. A stream ran through a sprinkling of trees down into the hollow. Beyond the trees, we could see a church and a handful of houses.

I said, 'Let's go down. We can find out if there's a short cut to Pentre. It's a longer way than I thought.'

We followed the stream down the side of the hill, through a gate which was weighted shut with a big stone. The stone hung from the gate by a piece of wire – a hole had been bored through it to take the wire and this made the stone look like a big doughnut hanging from a string. We took a drink at the stream and walked up to the church. There was no one about, only a goat tied to a stake on the side of the road. But the road bent sharply as we passed the church, and round the corner we came upon three men sitting on a wooden bench outside a public house called the Mason's Arms. As we got nearer one of the men shouted, 'Here they come. All in, and far from home.'

We recognised Jack Ragtime. He was sitting in the centre of the group. He had a hazel switch in his hand and a sprig of heather in his cap.

'Stop-turn at the Colliery,' I thought.

The man on his right was a collier too. The other man was a farmer, with a sheepdog lying almost out of sight underneath the seat. Ragtime stood up, and called through the open window, 'Three lemonades, landlord. Their tongues are hanging out.'

Jack Ragtime's pal, a small man with a dark square face and hair lying straight and flat across his forehead said, 'You better repeat that order, Jack.'

Ragtime put his head in at the window again. 'Three lemons!'

A man's voice called back, 'Lemonade, eh! Who you got out there?'

Ginger and I went into the bar to fetch the drinks. It was a cool room floored with big flagstones and covered with a sprinkling of sand. There were photographs of football teams all over the walls and, behind the bar, was a framed print of an old man in a red cloak. He was a tall old man with a white beard and piercing eyes. On his head there was a fox-skin with the tail hanging down his back. Underneath was a verse in Welsh with a lot of strange Latin words mixed in.

When we got outside Arthur was sitting on the seat with the others – they made room for us and went on with their talking.

The farmer was saying, 'The coalmines have spoiled the farms up in these hills. They've burrowed underneath them and taken all the goodness out of the soil. All the richness in the soil goes down with the water; drained away; tapped away, you can say, into the workings. Higher up in Brecon now, it's different. There's no tapped land up there, and the soil's got a bit of fat in it.'

He paused, and Ragtime said as he slapped the hazel switch against his leg, '*Duw!* I've never thought of it. I suppose there's something in it.'

'Something in it! I'm certain there is. Before the pits started you could get a living out of the land – I've heard the old people say they could fatten up cattle on some of these meadows. They couldn't do it now. But you've only got to look for yourself – how many good fields have gone back to the bracken, and how many farms have fallen into ruin? The land won't yield if it's worked under. Take anything away from it – natural it is – and you make it the poorer.' The farmer finished his drink and put his glass on the windowsill, 'But you've got enough troubles of your own without hearing mine.'

Ragtime grinned as they shook hands. 'Seth and me have no troubles. What more do you want than to be sitting down by here hearing the larks on a fine afternoon like this. We're on the right side of the mountain, aren't we, Seth?'

The farmer rose on his stick and whistled quietly between his teeth. The sheepdog got up lazily and followed him down the road.

As we watched them go round the corner, Ragtime said, 'There may be something in it. You can't take the guts out of the mountain without harming the skin.'

'Perhaps so,' answered Seth, 'but supposing it is – what do you call it – tapped soil, they get a good picking out of it, and he doesn't seem to look so bad living on John Jones' country.'

'A hard life though, Seth, and no stop-turns.'

'I wouldn't mind a dekko at it!'

'You must have the farming blood in you, Seth. Come up from the country to the Valleys you did?'

Seth shook his head. 'No, my father was a fisherman.' He turned to Arthur and asked him, 'How old are you, *bychan*?'

'Just under ten; ten in November.'

'I'd be about his age, perhaps a bit younger, when we moved up from Pembroke.'

'Bad times was it?' asked Ragtime.

'No, not worse than they were usually. No, I often heard my old man say how it was. He used to be out fishing for days at a time. Sometimes he would be away for weeks when he was working another part of the coast. Well, one day after a hard trip, they were sailing in close to the coast. It was a fair sunny day like this one, when you're certain you should be having a bigger kick out of life than you're getting. The old chap was watching the coast through his spying-glass and, just as they were passing a spot where the green fields came right down to the sea, he saw a man walking with his wife and two kids, strolling along contented, all in their best clothes. Then it came to him in a flash and he put down his spying-glass. "Why can't I be on shore enjoying myself with the family? Fool that I am!" As soon as he made port and got paid off, he vowed he'd never put to sea again, but would live with his wife and kids on shore like a proper man should. Well, the pits were opening, and there was talk of big money, and the old gent sold his sea-boots and up we moved. And...' he took off his cap and, looking round and nodding his head in all directions as though there was a big audience, 'Gentlemen, here I am!'

'Ay,' said Ragtime, 'and here for a bit we'll stay. *Lan a hi*, Seth.'

The landlord – an oldish man with a thoughtful face, came out and took the farmer's place on the bench. He wore a black denim jacket. Ragtime and Seth got up and went inside, and for a while the landlord sat smoking. He pointed out the air quivering above the sun-baked road, and when he had broken the silence I asked him who was the old man in the picture in the bar. He pulled his pipe slowly from his mouth and then said deliberately, 'That's a picture of old Dr Price of Llantrisant. Ever heard of him?'

Arthur said excitedly, 'Yes. My father knew him. He's told me a lot about him. When he was a boy he lived near Dr Price.'

'Who is your father, *bach*?'

'William Pritchard.'

'The Shop?' He tapped his pipe vigorously on the seat. 'Oh, your father and me are old butties – I was born in Pentyrch, the same as your father. Well, well. Like him in the face you are, the both of you. Your father and me have talked to the old doctor many times.'

The other two came back and Ragtime asked, 'Telling the lads about the picture, Davey?'

The landlord nodded, and Ragtime leaned over towards us, 'He didn't tell you how much he was offered for that photograph of Dr Price?'

We looked at the landlord who was smiling with amusement.

'No, he wouldn't tell you. But I'll tell you,' Ragtime said with emphasis. 'An American up here last summer offered ten pounds for that bit of a picture and Mr Lewis here wouldn't take it. Too much money you've got, Davey!'

The landlord said, 'Ay, that's the trouble no doubt, Jack. But I don't mind telling you this: if he offered me a hundred pounds I wouldn't have taken it.'

Ragtime argued, 'He was a good man was Dr Price. I grant you that, Davey, but that's a lot of money for a bit of a picture.'

Ginger had never heard of Dr Price and asked, 'Did he cure many people?'

The landlord said quietly, 'He was a good doctor, only fifty years before his time. If a man was ill with a bad stomach, he'd set to work to cure the man first and his stomach – if it still needed it – afterwards. He wasn't particular about the fee either.'

Ragtime agreed, 'He was a good doctor, Davey, no doubt about it, and on the side of the people.' Then he turned to us. 'Did you ever hear how he cured the young boy from Crumlin? Did you, Davey?'

Mr Lewis said, 'No, I can't say that I have. What is it, Jack?'

Seth interrupted, 'We better have another drink, Mr Lewis, before he starts, because if he gets going, it will be stop-tap before he finishes.'

The landlord went inside and returned with the beer.

Ragtime took a sip and started, 'This is a true story...'

Seth made a noise but Ragtime carried on without taking notice.

'About thirty years ago a man from Crumlin had a son – just like one of you boys by here now. Only this boy was wasting away. Nothing they gave him would turn into flesh, and he was like a reed that the wind was threatening to bend over. The father took him to the doctors down in Newport, and they all took a walk round him and said, "He's getting thin. Feed him up. Milk and eggs! Milk and eggs!" They gave the lad enough milk and eggs to start a shop with, but he still didn't put on flesh, though he had enough appetite to eat a horse between two bread vans. Then somebody told his father, "Take the lad over to Llantrisant – old Dr Price will cure him if anybody will." So he took his son down to Llantrisant, and although it was late when they got there, the doctor didn't keep them waiting. He had a look at the boy and asked his father a lot of questions like the doctors do, then he told him, "I'll cure your son if you do this one thing: take him home now and bring him back in three days' time, but from the time he leaves here till the time he returns he's not to touch a bite of anything to eat, and he's only to have a sip of water to drink." The father was a bit uncertain about this, because the lad was pretty thin already and three days on fresh air would take any stuffing he had left right out of him entirely, but he made up his mind suddenly and said, "I'll do it, doctor. It's his only chance!"'

'They went home and after three lean days he brought his son back. He had to carry him, just: the lad was on his last legs and ready to eat up anything he put his eyes on.

When Dr Price saw him he said, "Right! Well done, bring him into this room, by here." They went into a room with a big table covered with a white cloth – it was just an ordinary room except there was a big double-barrelled gun standing in the corner. Dr Price put the boy to sit up to the table facing the gun, and he told his father to sit alongside him. He told the lad he must do everything he said, and he warned the father to keep a close eye on his son. Then he rang a bell. A few seconds later a woman came in carrying a plate covered with a white cloth. Dr Price said, "Put it down on this side of the table, Mary." The woman left the room and the doctor uncovered the plate and showed one of the finest dinners that had ever been cooked on a Thursday, and the smell of it soon filled the room. The boy was almost starting out of his skin when he saw the meal in front of him, but Dr Price fixed him with his eye and said in a firm voice, "If you make one move towards the plate I'm going to shoot. Stay still where you are," and he put his hand on the gun. Then he said to the father, "Push the plate gently towards the boy." The father pushed the plate slowly across the table until it was right under the boy's nose, and he was staring at it as though he'd been hypnotised. As the plate came closer his mouth opened and closed just as though he were eating and his face showed the agony he was going through.'

Ragtime took a glance at us, as much as to say, 'Now I've got you where I want you.' Then he went on. 'In a minute the sweat began to show on the boy's forehead, and his jaw dropped and his mouth stayed open. Dr Price was watching him all the time. Then the boy started to shiver and the doctor said, "Hold it, *bach*. It won't be long now," and suddenly something dropped out of the boy's mouth on the plate and he screamed loud when he saw it. But Dr Price went over the other side of the table and lifted the boy off the chair onto the sofa, and said, "Well done, *bach*! Well done! You shall have a proper dinner now." Then he picked the thing off the table and examined it. It was a small lizard, and it had been slowly eating the boy away.'

He paused again for exactly the right length of time. 'Well, there's nothing to tell after that. Dr Price kept the lad and his father with him that night and he fed the lad up on the right things, and in the morning he was as fit again as a hare, though still a bit spare around the ribs. But he was strong enough to walk the fifteen miles back to Crumlin. The lad is still alive today, though getting on, of course. He's driving a bread van in Crumlin. He'll tell you that every word I've said is true – if you ask him.'

Seth said seriously, 'The first time I've heard that one, Jack, and I've heard a few of the doctor's doings.'

The landlord puffed at his pipe and smiled quietly, 'Who told you that one, Jack?'

'Oh, I heard it somewhere, Davey; a long time ago, before going into the army. I'm pretty good at remembering stories.'

'You are, but you sure that wasn't a homemade story now?'

Ragtime pretended to look hurt. 'Come now, Davey. Me, make it up? How could you expect a bloke like me to do that? It takes a poet to make a story now, doesn't it? And take a look at me: do I look like a bard?' He screwed up his face to his toughest fighting leer to disprove any claim they might give him to words.

The landlord chaffed him, 'Well, Jack, if you don't make them up, you know a good place to find them.'

He winked and answered, 'Perhaps so.'

After listening to Ragtime's story we told the men that we intended going to Pentre. They said we had come a long way off the road; we should have cut straight across the highest part of the hill, straight across the Roman road. If we continued in the direction we were going we would reach Caerphilly Castle, as Davey Lewis said; or the Boar's Head, Caerphilly, as Seth corrected him. It was too late to think of going so far and, as Ragtime and Seth were going down the hill, we decided to walk as far as the Garth Farm with them. We reached the tent before dusk, and Fatty and Nipper had made a huge fire and the supper was ready for cooking.

On our second night out it started to rain – the fine unceasing rain of the hills. The tent began to leak and the water to drop down inside the wall. When I awoke just after dawn and saw the rain dropping dismally off the fern-leaves, something inside told me that the holiday was at an end. Although the stores were already sodden with water and the bedclothes beginning to get damp, we still pretended that it would soon clear up.

Fatty said, looking out, 'This is like the day the Baptists chose for their Sunday school treat, but it will soon pass over.'

Ginger was wringing out his socks after walking a little way through the bracken. 'Ay, that's what the Baptists said, and it kept on raining nearly to the following year's treat.'

Fatty asked, 'Was it wet on St Swithin's day this year?'

'Yes, I can remember it. It started to rain just as we were going back to school in the afternoon. An old bloke on the road said, "Rain it is then – forty days and forty nights of it."'

'We'd better pack up then. There are about twenty days to go.'

Arthur pointed out, 'But it hasn't rained for the last three days. I think it's an old superstition.'

Fatty said piously, sticking up for Swithin, 'It may have rained in the night. We can't tell!'

After a meagre breakfast, we sat down to play a game called Pelmanism with a pack of cards, but after shifting around the tent, trying to dodge the drops of rain that kept appearing in new places of the roof, we gave up the cards and just watched the drops forming on the wall, wondering which drop would be the first to fall.

Outside the pound, a fine mist shut off the view of the opposite hill, and the long sheep-wall disappeared on our left into a grey curtain. The bleating of sheep we couldn't see somehow made things doubly melancholy.

Fatty was the first to weaken. 'What about going down for today? We could leave the tent and most of the things up here, and come back tomorrow when the rain stops.'

'But it will rain tomorrow according to your Swithin,' Ginger reminded him.

Fatty then came out into the open, 'Oh, let's go home anyhow, we're sitting around here like a lot of ducks without a pond.'

Arthur said, 'Wait you a bit, there'll soon be a pond.'

But we stayed a while after this, making no preparations to go, although it was now clear that the holiday was over. Then, just before noon, we broke camp silently. We wrapped up all the stuff together in crude bundles, and tied them to the poles, setting off in Indian file through the bracken. After we had gone a little way, we heard a whistle and a sheepdog came out of the mist to inspect us. Nipper was the only one who had enough spirit left to take notice of it.

Long before we came in sight of the valley we were soaked through, but our spirits rose a little when we saw the village.

Ginger said, 'It hasn't been so bad. We've slept out, and that's what we set out to do.'

'We have that!'

'And we'd have slept out for a fortnight if it hadn't been for the weather.'

In spite of the rain, I didn't want to go down into the valley. If we'd only had a tent that didn't leak, we could have stayed until the rain had passed. It surely wouldn't last for more than two days. We could have dug a channel round the tent and have been quite comfortable. As we lifted the bundles over the wooden fence that separated the moorland from the road leading down into the valley, I thought: this is the end of the adventure; once back into the valley we'll never get into the hills before the winter comes on; going back to the valley is going back to live in a long narrow room with high walls. Why couldn't we live on the hills? The Ancient Britons and the Romans must have lived up there – they'd left little to show that they'd been in the Valleys – and they must have been all the healthier for it. But the soft chuffing of the winding engine down below in the valley seemed to say persuasively, 'Coal, Coal.' The coal had lined the valley with houses and, while the coal was there, that's where the people would be. Yet, for me, the hills were freedom, and the valley was the shop, minding the cow, errands, difficult customers and, last of all, the new baby.

Down the road a horse and cart overtook us – it was Jenkins the Milk coming down from one of the farms. He stopped the horse and shouted, 'Where you been, boys? On the tramp? Wet you are. There's room for two and the baggage – jump in.'

We put the bundles in the bottom of the float and Arthur and Nipper went down with Mr Jenkins, the rest of us walked.

Ginger soon showed that he was already back in the valley. He said, 'I wonder how our whippet is running. He's in for a race down the Vale, next Saturday I believe.'

Fatty too. 'Our kid's got a new bike. I'll be able to pinch a few rides when he's in work.'

They were glad to see us at the house, and very soon we were back into the old routine for school holidays, and the jobs were falling on us as fast as the rain: Arthur to go to the field and fetch the cow in for milking; me to weigh maize and, if there was time, potatoes; and Nipper to mind the baby. I was quite satisfied with my job – it meant that I should be in the warehouse most of the afternoon and while I was weighing out the bags of corn I could have a good think about the camping: what we could do to make it better next year, and could we club up for a real tent? And perhaps I could read *The Gem* that was hidden in a bin under the barley-meal.

After about an hour, Nipper came out to the warehouse. I asked him how he managed to mind the baby for all that time. He said, 'It wasn't long. She's a fine little baby; I nursed her and rocked her a bit. She's beginning to say words, too. Our Dinah says I can take her for a walk in the pram tomorrow, if it's fine.'

I felt a little misgiving – had I been treating the baby unfairly? She couldn't be so bad after all – Nipper seemed to like her. She was growing up. That was it! She was growing into a little girl. I made up my mind to have a good look at that baby when I went in for tea.

Nipper helped me to weigh the maize. He scooped it out of the bin into the paper bags, while I weighed the bags and tied them up with string. We soon had a shelf full of neat parcels ready for the weekend. Then we started on the potatoes.

Father came out after we had weighed about two hundredweight. He said, 'You're getting along fine. That's the maize, is it?' He took two bags from the shelf, put the fourteen-pound weight on the scale and tested each bag separately. Nipper and I held our breath as the scale started to move but each time it balanced beautifully. 'Well done. You're weighing pretty accurately. Another sack of potatoes and you can sign off.'

When Father had gone we decided that we could enjoy a little rest with good conscience, and we dug down into the barley-meal until we found *The Gem*. But we hadn't been reading for long when we heard footsteps again in the yard outside. This time it was Tom – he had come out for a smoke. As he lit his cigarette, he said, 'I'm in a fix: old Mrs Wilkins Checkweigher wants her order up; she wants the tin of salmon for her old man's tea. It's too wet to turn out with the horse and cart – I shall wait until it slackens off. Will one of you take the salmon up?'

I liked walking in the rain, so I took off my canvas apron and put on a sou'wester and a mackintosh and started off. Just as I was going, Tom said, 'Call in at Mrs James Incline Top and ask her if she wants any corn up this weekend.'

The water was pouring out of the drainpipes and there was a small stream in the gutter – it carried an empty matchbox which I placed in it, right from the top of the street to the bottom. There was no hurry and it didn't matter if the salmon tin did get wet.

When at last I reached Mrs Wilkins' house, she raised her hands when she saw me. 'I thought I was never going to get it in time. There's good you are to bring it up in the rain.' She was smiling now – for a reward – but she was only doing it with her mouth that made the case of a smile, with nothing real inside it. She came out of the doorstep and held out one of her hands. 'But there, the rain is stopping now and we'll soon be having a rainbow. It won't be so bad for you going back.'

I was glad I was not living in Mrs Wilkins' house. She had no children and spent nearly all the day cleaning and polishing. Her husband was a quiet man with a long neck, and she wore his trousers and his pants. He couldn't put a foot on the carpet in the house, and she'd hardly let him go upstairs to bed for fear of smudging the linoleum. When he came in – except on very special occasions – he went in round the lane and through the back, and he had to take his boots off and leave them out by the wash-house like they are supposed to do in China.

Incline Top was the highest row of houses in the valley. The houses clung to the side of the hill, and if you stood at the end of the short garden at the back you were higher than the chimney itself. Mrs James, where I was to call, kept a lot of chickens. They roamed about the mountain behind the house, but she had trained them well to lay their eggs in the right place. Her husband had hurt his back in the pit and couldn't get out of bed. I liked going to this house, because if Mrs James asked you, 'Would you like a cup of tea and a slice of cake?' you knew she meant you to say yes. There was a steep garden at the front of the house, filled with redcurrant and gooseberry bushes. The house itself was built long before the pits came, and only had two rooms downstairs. In the bigger room – the front room – was the bed. It was downstairs to save Mrs James' legs, and with the grandfather clock and the chest of drawers it filled the room.

Old Mr James was anchored to the bed like an old barge that used to be half sunk down in the canal. He was propped up with pillows so that he was almost sitting up but, like the old barge, he seemed to be sinking lower in the bed each time you saw him. He always wore his waistcoat and muffler over his flannel shirt, and to look at him you'd think he'd been out walking and had suddenly come home and jumped into bed, just from a whim. I could never find out whether he had his trousers on. But he'd been in bed for years, and the doctor said he'd never leave it, at least not on his legs.

Mrs James was unusual to look at, too. She was a tall woman with an oval, yellowish face and she wore a strip of red flannel round her head and over her ears for some complaint she had. Her waist was so high that it was nearly under her armpits and she wore men's boots because of the heavy work she did.

The rain had stopped by the time I reached the house and, as I climbed up the steep garden through the fresh-smelling bushes past a border of thyme and marjoram, I saw that the front door was open. This was a house you could enter without knocking – there'd always be a welcome. But today, as I got near the door, I looked inside and stopped on the threshold. Mr James was lying in bed almost flat out. He had a clean shirt on and his hair was flattened down and parted, and his hands were outside the quilt. At the side of the bed there was a preacher kneeling and praying, and Mrs James was standing by the chest of drawers, weeping quietly. I looked at the old man's face. His eyes were closed and his face looked peaceful. He's dead! He's dead! I told myself in a panic, and my mouth went dry and a lump came into my throat because I'd never seen a dead man yet. And I was turning to go back hurriedly, but Mrs James looked up and smiled and motioned me to wait in the garden.

Soon afterwards, I heard Mrs James' voice – stronger than usual – and then the preacher, Mr Hughes the

Congregational, came down the path and raised his walking stick as he left. Mrs James called me in, and asked me to sit on the bottom of the bed.

The old man was more alive, and much brisker, than he'd been for a long time. He talked so quickly that his wife hardly had a chance to give me the list of things she wanted sent up. When I had finished taking the order down she made tea and, while we were drinking, the old man told me about the village before the pits and of the road running across the top of the mountain. Some people said it was a Roman road because all the stones were laid in the Roman fashion, but Mr James said that the road was built for the pack mules to bring down the iron from Merthyr.

Before I left, Mrs James gathered a bunch of thyme and marjoram for me to take home, and as I was going out through the door the old man called out from the bed, 'You bring that brother of yours up for a chat the next time you come; the scholar. What's his name?'

'Arthur?'

'That's right. Me and him can bring up old times and set a few things right between us.'

After I'd been in a house like the James' I thought: there's something to be said for living in a shop, in spite of customers like Mrs Wilkins and in spite of working on a Saturday.

Before going to bed that night I had quite made up my mind about the baby. It was as if she had changed suddenly in the short time we had been away. When we left, I thought of her not as one of the family, but as something that went into the cot and that had to be fed at stated times, even before the boys. How many times had we waited for the baby to be seen to first! But when we returned I saw her as she was – a member of the family in her own right. She captured me in spite of myself. Her blue eyes and fair skin, and especially the way she smiled, even when I slyly looked at her with a scowl. I said to Dinah that evening, after she came downstairs from putting the baby to bed, 'I've oiled the wheels of the pram and I've put the brakes right. Do you think I could take the baby for a ride tomorrow just to see how it runs?'

Dinah asked, 'Do you really mean it?'

I nodded my head frowning, half ashamed that I was giving in, and she laughed.

'Well! It must be the mountain air. It's done you good. You've really noticed the baby.' Then she said seriously, 'But I'd forgotten, David is taking her out tomorrow – I promised him this afternoon. You'll have to share the honour with your brother, Sir,' she added, mocking me.

But it had become a very important thing that I should get to know the baby, and I couldn't wait another day before taking her out. I said, 'Nipper and I can wheel her in turns.' As I took off my boots and slid them under the couch, I felt much happier about the baby because no longer would I have to pretend that I didn't like her. She would grow up into a pretty little girl and, when she was old enough, we could take her to the pictures and to the fair, and perhaps to the circus if it ever came back.

I said 'Goodnight' and started to climb the stairs, but almost as soon as I closed the door I heard Dinah's voice and I listened to her telling Mother, 'Fancy Willie wanting

105

to take the baby out. Our Willie is a funny boy...' the voice stopped short and the door at the bottom of the stairs flew open, and light flooded out. I scuffled up the stairs, but not quick enough to escape Dinah, who called out, 'He's still on the stairs. You cheat! Get off to bed, quickly! I knew he was listening.'

The bed that night, after sleeping on the ground, was as soft and as yielding as swansdown. I floated on it, and the feeling was so strange that I didn't want to sleep but to lie, enjoying the smoothness of the sheets and the warm tingle on the skin. My thoughts raced over all that happened during the past few days, and sharp pictures came up unsummoned and vanished when I tried to hold them; the darkness of the room became peopled with friendly figures and was a stage for delightful happening – some actual, and some painted with the deft brush of desire.

I thought suddenly of a sentence I had once read in a book: '*Who would play with the wind, let him not go seeking it.*' Playing with the wind! That is what we had been doing for the last few days up on the mountain. We had camped just to be able to boast that we had slept out at night in the teeth of the threat of darkness, and we had played with the wind.

The words made me restless and I sat up in bed too wide awake to think of sleep. I noticed that the room had become lighter; full of a soft white glimmer, as though around its walls there was a frieze of glow-worms, as brilliant as the one we had seen in the bracken. Looking out through the window I saw the moon, full but sliced in half by the curving top of Mynydd Leyshon. I watched it rising slowly until it was poised right on the top of the hill, dangerously poised, as if at any moment it would tumble down the slope into the valley. After getting up to look at the silver slates of the housetops and the knife-edged shadows of the chimneys, wondering that the moon could change the valley so completely into a scene out of a book, something not real, I got into bed unwillingly and went to sleep. But before the morning my mind had prolonged the scene so that it would have no ending. I dreamed that the moon had really come down into the valley, floating down as light as a soap bubble until it rested in Jenkins the Milk's green field at the bottom. There it shone quietly but powerfully until it tumbled all the people out of their beds and their houses. Gabbling with excitement they crowded down to Jenkins' field, climbing over his gates and jumping over his hedges. They formed a big circle with the moon in the centre, but no one dared touch it for fear they would become transparent, and the world could see what they were thinking. And they began to wonder at the moon, and to discuss how it came there and what they were going to do with it, until there arose a great babble and confusion. For, after the first amazement, everyone had different ideas about what was to be done with the moon, though nearly all were agreed that something would have to be done about it. They argued and shouted and wrestled and ran about, sometimes coming together in big groups and sometimes scattering all over the field like a host of dim-sighted ants, until all hope of agreement was gone. All the while the moon skimmed the surface of the field and shone peacefully. But, at last, when all the scurrying was finished, the people found themselves in four groups; each group believing that their way of dealing with the moon was the right way. The groups went into the four corners of the field to talk over their plans and to strengthen themselves for carrying them out.

In one corner was Watkins the Tailor – a deacon from the chapel. He gathered a lot of people about him, and they were all dressed in black with long faces and a smell of mothballs about them. With his long scissors in his hand, Watkins kept cutting the air and talking at the people. He told them that the moon's descent into the valley was a trick of the Devil, and the sooner they got the moon out again the better for everyone, because the moon was a friend of pagans and the first ally of the Devil and, if she stayed, fire and brimstone would eat up the land. All the people in black applauded him by saying, 'Hear, Hear,' many times, and '*Bendigedig*,' which means 'Blessed'.

In the second corner of the field was Mr Ebenezer the preacher, himself. He held up his hand and talked about the moon as if she were a young girl, and told the people that they should be glad to welcome her to the valley, and that since she had chosen to rest in Jenkins' field, there she should stay – he would answer for Jenkins, who was a faithful and willing member of the chapel. She would become an ever present reminder of the wonders of Creation, and the honour singled out for their little community. The people murmured in deep agreement.

In the third corner was Jack Ragtime with the colliers and the people who never went to chapel, and Jack was saying, 'Well, butties, this is the best thing that could have happened to this valley. Light now all the year round, in a place where there has been a good bit of darkness. There's something about the moon that's a bit homely to me. She's like a big collier's lamp that never wants oil or trimming. Perhaps this is a sign of the better times they are always promising the miners. So this is what I propose: we should give the old gel a real Valleys welcome. Tomorrow we'll hold a 'sports' with foot and whippets and trotters if we can manage it, and tomorrow night, when she should be shining top-of-her-form, we'll roll a few barrels of beer down into Mr Jenkins' backyard and we'll drink to the moon, and we'll show her she's come to a place where they know how to treat a stranger. Then we'll sing, till she knows that she's made no mistake and has come into the valley she intended to.'

In the fourth corner there was a small band of people – mostly women – all with their backs to the moon and all talking noisily. Mrs Wilkins Checkweigher was the noisiest of them all. She was saying that she didn't believe it was the moon at all but that it was some trick those old advertising men were up to, and that Jack Ragtime and his butties had been bribed with beer to act up to it. Their talk was loud and long, but it amounted to nothing, for they couldn't agree even amongst themselves.

After the four parties had been for a long time in their corners, they gathered together again in the big circle. Then they decided that each party should send a leader to the centre space of the circle, and that there he should preach to the moon. And the one who could preach best, standing before its light, should decide what was to be done with it.

Jack Ragtime was first, and he pushed his cap to the back of his head and made a speech like a poet, so that the moon began to wax in her shining. Then came Mrs Wilkins Check, who only nagged at her until her face was covered over with a shadow. Mr Ebenezer was next, and with a voice of music he preached better than in any sermon, but the light of the moon seemed to dazzle him. Then came, last of all, Watkins the Tailor; the deacon with the long scissors. He started off quietly holding the scissors to his side but gradually using it to cleave and snip the air, he reached a white-hot *hwyl* and, throwing back his head, stared full at the moon's face. Some say he had his eyes shut, but he argued and shouted and persecuted the moon, until there was no strength left in him and he was like a plant that had lost all his sap. It was plain that Watkins' band would decide what was to be done with her, for when he had finished their 'Hear, Hears,' and '*Bendigedig*' came thicker and faster than hail, and no one dared their frenzy.

So Watkins stood in the centre of the field over against the moon, tearing his hair with one hand and pointing at the moon repeatedly with his scissors, shouting in a hoarse voice, 'Roll her to the sea. Roll the pagan to the sea. To the sea! *I'r mor a hi.*'

And the men in black, the long-faced men and the sour, put their shoulders to the moon and strained with a mad fervour until they got her rolling. She moved heavily now so that the long-faced men had to push hard at each step while Jack Ragtime and his boys kept pinching their backsides to distract them. But they kept the moon moving, chanting their '*Bendigedig*' the whole time, till the moon rolled softly past Nantgarw, Gwaelod-y-Garth, Pentre-Twym, and on into the sea.

When they reached there, the sour-faced men stood on the cliff, more dead now than alive, to watch the last plunge of the moon into the sea. But she floated gently down and, bouncing over the water, she became a small ball in the distance, throwing back a long lane of silver.

Now, whenever the moon looks over the top of Mynydd Leyshon she seems to have a smile to herself and the grim-faced men then know that the time has come for them to hide their heads and to mutter their '*Bendigedig*', but only very quietly under their breaths.

I didn't like hearing that someone had died – it woke a quick fear that was there all the time but only came into mind when I heard of a death. I walked round two streets to avoid a house where I knew there was someone lying dead, and a dog howling sent a thrill of fear through me. Once, when I saw through an open window the feet of a corpse about to be put in a coffin, the picture of the grey woollen socks sticking out from a shroud stayed with me for months and came up again and again with frightening clearness. Then they asked me to go to the funeral of a boy from my class at school; they wanted me to be one of the bearers. I said I wouldn't go, and they tried to persuade me.

Father said, 'You'll have to learn to like going to funerals.'

I said, 'I never shall.'

'Wouldn't you like someone to come to your funeral, if you died?'

The thought sent me into a white panic, but I replied obstinately, 'I wouldn't want a funeral. You could throw me on the ashpit. Funerals are all wrong.'

Then Father said, 'I can see you're a follower of Dr Price – you'd like to be burnt up on the top of the mountain.'

'It would be better than a funeral. I think I would.'

I was glad they didn't expect me to go to the funeral of Uncle Tom's wife. She died at the beginning of that winter and her funeral passed along the road that runs along the foot of the hill behind our house. Mother told me to watch for it – there would be a hearse and four coaches. Nipper and Arthur stood on the wall at the back, while I stood in the yard, wishing and not wishing to see it. Nothing came for a long time and I went inside to polish the brass on the harness.

After a while I heard Nipper shout excitedly, 'Here it is, quick. You can just see the top of the coaches.'

The horses were tired after pulling up from Pontygwaith and the black coaches moved slowly through a mist that was coming down from the hill. It looked sad, but I watched the funeral as though from a great distance and nothing of me took part in it.

Late that afternoon, a lot of people called at our house on the way home. We saw near-relations we had never heard of, and we looked in awe at a family which had spread, all in one afternoon, over four wide and important valleys. They crowded to the table in relays, and then poured out into the yard to stand talking in groups. And, for us who listened, drifting from one group to another, it was like hearing the history of the family recited by its chief members. But Uncle Tom, who would have been at the front of the stage, wasn't present and the pageant was greyer and less exciting than it would have been.

We didn't see him until a month afterwards. Then Father sent me down on a Saturday evening to ask him to come up to dinner on the following day. A niece was keeping house for him, but she had gone home and he was alone when I called. He folded up the newspaper he was reading as I walked in and, taking off his spectacles, rose briskly to his feet.

'So it's you, Willie. How are you? Sit by the fire there. I'm glad to see you, boy.'

As I sat down I looked at him quickly to see if he had changed, but to the eye he was the same – his moustache standing out fiercely, and his movements as quick and as clear-cut as ever. He was in his waistcoat and was wearing no collar and tie – unusual for a Saturday night, when he had always gone out to strengthen himself against the coming of Sunday.

'All keeping well up there?' he asked.

'Yes, thanks. How is the work going, Uncle Tom?'

He had been leaning forward with his forearms resting on his knees, a little tense. When I asked this question he relaxed into the chair and said pleasantly, 'Well! You're asking a difficult thing now, boyo.'

It was a relief for him to talk about something remote from his real thoughts. He filled his pipe carefully and, after lighting it, his words poured out as into a smooth channel where before they had been long dammed, made sluggish by the landslide that had suddenly cut across his

113

life. 'Twenty years ago they mined coal. There was an art in it. Now they drag it out like a clumsy midwife bringing on a delivery. Get it out. Get it out at all costs – let the devil take care of the consequences. And he nearly always does. Now in the district where I work...'

I was glad that I had asked the right question. His eyes lit up and he slipped easily into the stories of the coalfield; the disputes and the strikes, the crusade for the minimum wage, and the moulding of men who would become a legend as strong and enduring as the legend of King Arthur.

The fire shone in his face and made his hair glisten, and the story he was relating fell away and he suddenly stood, as it were, out of time – an old prophet, a *jongleur* of olden times, a bard of the Court; an old man sitting beside the fire and weaving a tale of unyielding toil and struggle which broke men but never their spirit.

'The miners,' he went on, 'will have their day. Never doubt that. They've soaked their bread in their own sweat for long enough. Every day the struggle is making them more able to win what is their right. And they've been in darkness for too long to be frightened by the colour of the pitch of hell or what will happen if they try to take what is their due. They'll have their day!'

His voice had risen and he spoke with an emotion far above his usual style. He finished abruptly, a little ashamed that he had shown something of his real self; a quick glimpse through his hard, mocking front to the world. Then he slumped back into the chair and, as he stared into the fire, his whole body seemed to say, 'Words, words. Fine words! But will they cure the ache in you?' But he got up, quickly throwing off the humour like a damp cloak from his shoulders. He tapped his pipe on the hob of the grate, and said with a shake of his head, 'Living alone, *bychan*, is no life at all. A man without his wife is like a tree without roots: nothing at all to steady him against the wind.' Then he took his snuff out of his waistcoat pocket and held it out to me with the old knowing look in his eye. 'Have a pinch?'

He was surprised when I accepted, and grinned like his old self. 'That's the way. Clears the head.' I took a pinch and sniffed it very cautiously. He watched me closely and his face creased up as the tears began to flood into my eyes. He promised to come up on the following day and as I left he said, 'So long now. I'll be up middling prompt. Mind you get enough potatoes peeled.'

As I walked home there was a long line of fire spreading across the hills. The flames kept spurting out and dying down, only to flare up again. Here and there, quick-moving figures could be seen against the glow. They moved purposefully, and shortly afterwards fires would break out in a different place further along the hill. The boys were setting fire to the bracken. They would be the ones who had just left school and had started work in the pit – Jack Morgan and his pals. But the hill looked as if it had suddenly taken a glowing crown, and the valley was full of light and the sharp smell of burning bracken. The stars were cold-seeming and very far away above the flaming hill. It was strange, looking at the valley in the flickering light of the fires, to think how it was close-huddled with people in the dark shadows that were houses; and men walking, working, singing and swearing half a mile underneath. Tonight the hills did not overpower but gave protection, strong ramparts against an outer darkness. I remembered with wonder how I felt after the camp, that it was not right to live down in the valley. But I wasn't the same, although it was only two months ago; the sap and the bark were changing.

PART III

After the holidays, life was very calm until we began to have trouble with the cow. In the summer, the cow stalked across each day like one of Jacob's spectral kine. Not that she was thin – indeed, she was very fat – but at any time she was likely to cause us trouble, and often did.

We had two fields by the river for grazing the horse and cow. They were small pieces of land squeezed into long strips by the hills. It was one of our jobs in the summer to change over the animals from one field into another – you rode the horse and he went at any pace you liked, but the cow only had one speed and nothing could alter it. When you were in a hurry she still plodded along very slowly, her back legs splaying, her udder banging from side to side, and her tail swinging like the pendulum of a very leisurely clock. Then she was always getting lost. She charged through the hedge like a tank whenever she saw a nice patch of grass growing outside in the lane, and no amount of barbed wire would stop her. Then she wandered off, and it would take two of us an hour or so to find her.

One day shortly after we returned, she got out of the bottom field. Arthur and I spent the afternoon looking for her in the usual places, but we could find no trace of her. Then we met Ginger Williams. He was wheeling a barrow full of potatoes from his garden, and when he saw us he sat down on the handle of the barrow and waited till we came up. He asked us, 'Looking for your cow? She was up on Jenkins' farm and he's playing hell because she was in with the cattle eating up his grass.'

'Where's she now?'

'Jenkins turned her out. She was standing by an allotment looking over the fence when I came down.'

We would have liked to talk with Ginger because we hadn't seen him since the camping, but I said, 'C'mon, Arthur, we'd better go up for her. Perhaps we can catch her before she does the damage.'

Ginger grinned as we hurried off and called from his seat on the barrow, 'It was Thomas the Teacher's allotment. She was looking hard at his cabbages.'

We climbed through two steep streets and up through Incline Top, asking everyone we met, 'Have you seen our cow? She's a brown one with a white face and the map of Spain on her neck.'

A girl told us, 'I saw her this morning eating the top of Mrs Lewis's privet.'

Arthur said to me, 'The privet won't be the end of it, I'm

thinking. She's having a day out.' And then, after taking a short cut through the lane up to the top where the houses finished, he said in his serious way, 'Don't you think milk out of a tin tastes just as nice as cow's milk?'

I said, 'Oh, it won't be so bad when the winter comes. The cow will be in the stall most of the time then.'

'Yes, it's better in the winter – cutting up mangel-wurzels is easier than chasing over the mountain for her. But I still think that a cow is not...' he stopped and pointed, and said in a smaller voice, 'necessary, I was going to say.'

We had reached the open land above the houses, where there was a row of allotments opened up during the war. The cow was in the middle of them. As we got nearer we could see the gap in the hedge through which she had broken in. She had waded right into the middle of the first allotment she came to. She had tried some onions and had turned down part of a row of runner beans, but her main attack had been on the red cabbages. She was eating her way towards the end of the last row. We stopped and watched her for a few moments, hardly believing she could have eaten so much, She saw us and raised her head and looked at us with brief interest. She was swollen to a tremendous size and Arthur began to doubt whether she could come out by the same gap in the hedge.

'She got in that way, and that's the way she's coming out, even if we've got to get behind and push her out!'

I took a stick from the wreckage of the row of beans and went round the other side of her, and shouted and raised the stick. Between us we managed to get her out, though not without ruining a bed of parsley which she scattered in her final charge through the gap.

After she was safely outside, we walked round the garden trying to count up the damage. Arthur said, 'That'll be a couple of pounds at least. But it isn't the cost! Old Thomas will be as wild as an Indian when he gets to know.'

'Father will be wild too. Is Mr Thomas still on holiday?'

Arthur grinned, 'Yes. Perhaps the garden will pull round a bit by the time he gets back. A drop of rain will do a world of good, you know.'

'Maybe, but he'll have to go cadging if he wants to pickle any cabbage this year.'

We stirred up the cow and started home. While we were talking she had been munching the grass on the verge of the road as if the day's business of feeding had just begun.

On our way down through the streets, two women stopped their gossiping and turned with folded arms to look at us. They stared at us as if we were the front part of a travelling circus. One of the women called out, 'There's big she is! Is she calving, boy? Any chance of a bit of veal later on, now?'

I shook my head, and Arthur too – which was unusual – didn't have words to lay his tongue to.

We took her down for Tom to milk her, but she was so bloated that she could hardly get in through the stable door. As soon as we had fastened the chain around her neck, she started to munch some hay that had been left in her manger. Tom came out and we told him what had happened, and he grinned when he saw the cow. 'She made a meal of it, by the look of her. Poor old Thomas! He was proud of his cabbages. It would spoil his holidays if he knew.'

Tom went into the shop and brought Father out. He looked serious and said a few sharp words about keeping the fence in proper repair. Mr Thomas the Teacher was a good customer and couldn't be offended. Father asked, 'When does Mr Thomas come back?'

'Mrs Thomas is sending a card a day or two before they're due.'

'Remind me, Tom. I'll go up and see him myself.'

After Father had gone, the news got to the house and Nipper came out, and then Mother. She talked to the cow and scolded her for getting into trouble. But the cow looked round in her mild way, chewing the cud all the time, her conscience as white as the milk she would soon be giving in the pail.

By the next morning the stir caused by the cow's wanderings had diminished like her girth, but Arthur and I were just at the beginning of their sequel. First of all there was the gap in Thomas's garden to be closed up, and then the hedge of the Bottom Field to be seen to; the breach to be filled in, and the other weak places to be strengthened. We had a good pair of hedging gloves, and mending the hedge was a new and interesting job. We had plenty of barbed wire and all the tools to dig a hole to drive a post in. We spent the whole day doing the job, taking some lunch down in a small bag. Everything seemed to be ending happily, at least for us.

Mr Thomas had not returned from Cardigan yet. When he did return, Father went up straightway to see him. We were having supper when Father came back from the interview and we could see by the way he came in, asking briskly if there was anything good, that he and Thomas had settled things up.

When he had sat down and was drinking a cup of tea, Mother asked him, 'What did Mr Thomas think about the garden?'

Father put his cup down carefully. 'Well, now, he couldn't think much of the garden, could he? But we settled up fine.'

'How much?'

Father liked fencing with questions. 'Mr Thomas said, "Of course it couldn't be helped – an act of God." And Mrs Thomas was quite merry about it. She even admitted that the loss of the cabbage would save him from indigestion. He would eat pickled cabbage for supper when it didn't suit him. He suffers...'

But Mother asked him again, cutting across his words, 'Come on, Pa, how much?'

Father took another drink of his tea and put the empty cup down. He looked meaningly at it and Mother gave a sigh and poured him another. Then he grinned and said, '*Diolch yn fawr*. How much, did you say? Five shillings.'

'Five shillings! That was cheap.'

Arthur and I looked at one another and we both saw the shattered row of beans and the blighted cabbages. It was cheap. But Father added casually from behind his cup, 'And a pint of milk every evening for a month.'

What was that? Arthur and I sat up in our chairs. 'Oh!'

'Who suggested that?' Mother asked.

'Well, I did, my girl. And it settled the business

122

straightway. I told Thomas it would be like making the old cow pay for the damage herself, and give her her due, she gives good milk. Mrs Thomas said, "Yes indeed, no doubt. She's well fed." "Right," said Thomas, "that's a bargain, Mr Pritchard, and it's bread and milk instead of pickled cabbage for supper." Mrs Thomas said, "Yes, and a better man you'll be for it."'

Father was very pleased with the settlement, for Mr Thomas was quite ready to forget about the disaster. But Arthur and I were looking across the table at one another with serious faces and asking ourselves: and who would be taking Thomas his supper every night? One of the boys! And one of the boys would have to walk with a can of milk halfway up the mountain to the loneliest part of the village, and not a street lamp to keep him from stumbling over a sheep that had strayed on the road. It wasn't a good settlement, we were certain of that. And if you asked us squarely, we would have told you that we preferred that Mr Thomas lived another winter with his indigestion than that we should be burdened with the curing of it. We went to bed that night with a long view of dismal evenings carrying milk, and it was hard not to put the blame on the cow, who was surely the fountain of this new misfortune.

Yet, after we'd been taking the milk for a week, each of us doing the journey in turn, we thought nothing of it. It was just one of those things that looked bigger and more terrible than they really are – a monster on the skyline at dusk, but only a misshapen tree when you approached it. And then again, there was really something to interest us on the way up.

One night I had taken Nipper up with me for company, and I'd just shown him the trick of swinging the open can of milk right round at arm's length without spilling any, when we saw a courting couple coming towards us. In the darkness the form of the girl was familiar and we both stopped after they had passed.

Nipper whispered excitedly, 'Our Dinah!'

It looked like Dinah to me, but I'd never seen her with a boy. No, it couldn't be. She always said boys didn't interest her. 'Are you sure?' I asked Nipper.

'Sure it was. I can tell by the way she walks – as if she's got springs in the heels of her shoes!'

'Who was the chap?'

'I'm not sure, but I thought it was John Prosser – the chap who plays the organ in the Congregational.'

John Prosser! We were both silent, picturing the lean-faced collier of that name. At last Nipper gave judgment: 'Oh, he's all right. But fancy our Dinah!'

We agreed to say nothing about the meeting and went up each night hoping to see them again, but Dinah was too busy to do much courting, and we didn't see her a second time. Yet we were anxious to find out whether she knew that we shared her secret, and one night when she was scurrying us off to bed, standing at the bottom of the stairs as usual while we walked in slow procession to the top, Nipper, who was last, whispered down tauntingly, 'John Prosser. John Prosser. We saw you!'

She was off her guard for a moment, but she recovered and ran upstairs in time to catch us on the landing. 'You little monks! If you say a word about that, I'll make it hot for you.' She pretended to be angry and perhaps she really was, a little.

The days grew shorter and it was dark before we got home from school. Towards the end of the afternoon, the hill would stand out sharp-edged against the sky, and from the classroom window we could see a rock jutting out like a black pier over the valley. The four-twenty train slid down the incline, its whistle screaming shrilly as it passed the school. This afternoon, with all its windows aglow, it was a quick-moving chain of light. Darkness poured down early from the hills. Mr Thomas the Teacher put the lights on for the last lesson and the classroom became new – there were two big gas-standards at the front, and the back of the class was in shadow. But the blackboard shone and made it hard to read anything from it, so we had to change our lesson. Mr Thomas decided to give us an extra half-hour's singing.

In the new light, with the shadows of the desk making queer patterns and the yellow chrysanthemums on the mantelpiece suddenly becoming alive, we forgot we were in school and sang as though we had been translated to a high-vaulted cave, hewn out around a precious pool of light. Mr Thomas played on the piano and, after a while, we sang songs we had already learned. We would have sung until midnight. We rose with the music and breathed pure sound. Good singing! Good singing! But just after we had finished a beautiful lullaby, and were in that soft trance-like reaction that follows good achievement, we heard a scuffle of feet in the corridor, and then the 'home-time' bell clanged harshly, shattering the spell into countless little fragments. The class sighed and asked for another song but, wisely, Mr Thomas shook his head because he knew we could not now sing as well. We left school that afternoon reluctantly – a rare thing – carrying home a luminous memory of the singing.

We looked forward to the dark evenings since they brought new games and new delights. In the streets we could play 'Dicky-Show-Your-Light'. We chased 'Dicky' – who had a torch and who was bound to show it when we called. There was 'Weak Horses, Strong Donkeys' – a vigorous game played under a street lamp; and the risky, though thrilling, sport of stuffing a rainpipe with paper and setting a match to it. We waited out of reach for the hollow dismal note that went up as the paper took fire, and brought the householder in alarm to the door.

At home there was the warehouse where we could read without being disturbed. We shut the door and lit a small oil-stove and, sitting on a sack of meal, we read and talked until we were called from the house, or until the oil had burned out in the stove and the candle had guttered itself away.

Nos Calan Gaeaf – All Hallow'een – was a gay evening that year. We were all allowed to stay up late to supper, and the fun started as soon as the shop was closed. First of all came the 'Ducking Apple'. Mother placed three big apples in a bowl of cold water and we had to get them out without using our hands. Everyone had a try, and Tom got his apple out after a few seconds – but he had a big mouth. The rest of us coughed and spluttered about, flooding the room with water, but we only got a piece of green apple-skin between us. Arthur was the nearest. He got the apple against the side of the bowl, but he had to come up for a breath before he could get his teeth into it properly. Since the bowl gave us nothing, we tried biting at an apple that was threaded with a string and hung from a hook in the ceiling. Nipper had the most out of the apple on the string. He got on a chair and bent over with tilted head. Then he made the apple swing gently, taking a well-timed bite at it whenever it came near his open mouth.

Dinah came in with her boy. She was courting now – it was recognised, and there was no teasing her on the sly. John Prosser was short and lively and ready for a bit of fun, and it wasn't long before we got him to put his head in the bowl. He got an apple, but he had to duck hard for it. When he came up, we pretended we couldn't find the towel for him to wipe his face and he had to hold his head over the bowl for the water to drip off.

Nipper said at last, 'There it is,' and held the towel out of his reach – his eyes were too full of water to see – so that he was feeling round blindly and saying, 'Where? Where?' Everyone laughed and shouted, 'Here, here! Can't you see it?' John Prosser took the fun in good part and showed that he was equal to the comment Nipper had made on him: 'Oh, he's all right. He showed me the proper way to hold a marble taw that will knock ten out of the ring at the same time.'

When all the apples had gone from the bowl and only a gnawed stump was left swinging on the string, we stopped for supper. As we sat down, Mother said, 'Wait, there's a surprise!' and she placed a big dish of baked apples on the table, their skins golden-brown and glistening with sugar and butter.

That winter, too, I first smoked a cigarette. Before, with Ginger Williams, I had smoked dried leaves down by the river – we had been bathing and we lit a fire and gathered the leaves and rolled them into a piece of notepaper. The dried leaves made us cough and we agreed they weren't worth collecting. Later on, we decided to try some cigarettes. I took a packet of 'Cinderella' from the shop and, after dark one evening, we crawled into a dry culvert under the road. The stones had been washed clean by the rain water. We brought a candle – Ginger, Fatty and I.

The smoking was a rite, and we sat close together in the stone-arched culvert like conspirators. We experimented with the cigarettes and practised blowing out smoke through the nose. When each of us had passed this test – Fatty and I after a lot of tears in the eyes and tickling in the throat – we tried 'drawing in'. Ginger was the only one who could do it. He held his cigarette like a man who had been smoking for years. Fatty said that you could make smoke come out from your ears, but he couldn't tell how it was done, nor did he have the courage to try it, especially after he had tried to imitate the boys who had left school, holding the cigarette in the corner of his mouth, and blinding himself for some minutes when the smoke curled up and got into his eyes.

We crawled out of the culvert a little later, and I felt the two remaining cigarettes in my pocket without enthusiasm. Fatty didn't think much of it either. But Ginger said it was much better when you got used to it. Smoking was all right, but it was chewing like his father did that he couldn't stomach.

The miners had been on strike for three months, and Father was very worried because there was no money coming in; only the teachers and the farmers could pay. He stood behind the counter with his apron folded up at one corner, watching the men walking up and down the street. We daren't ask him for money to go to the pictures. He got irritable, easily annoyed, and home was not a good place to be in. There were no more happy evenings. The strike lay over the valley like a thick cloud that had frozen all movement and most mirth. There was no weekend bustle in the streets; there was no pay-day; only a slow torpid stream of men throughout the week walking the roads or slowly pushing their barrows of coal-pickings from the slag-heap on the hillside.

There were meetings, two or three times a week, in the Workmen's Hall, and then the slow pulse of life quickened. The streets were crowded with men discussing and arguing far into the night. The policemen walked in threes and they were very respectful when they asked the men standing about to move on. In the chapel on Sunday, Mr Ebenezer talked about God and Mammon – how each man must choose whom he is to serve. Jack Ragtime went to hear Mr Ebenezer preach – he had a respect for him, and, like a few more during the strike, he had taken to going to chapel occasionally – and we heard him telling Father afterwards, when he sold us some coal, that Mr Ebenezer had not left them much of a choice, although it was a very good sermon, one of his best. Because he was pretty sure that

God hadn't counted for much in the valley – at least, not since the coal came – and now Mammon had folded up his rickety stall these three months since and sloped off, like a trickster who'd been doing good business with the three-card trick and suddenly makes his getaway.

After the first month of the strike, the soup-kitchen opened at school and they used our classroom for the dining-hall. I asked Ginger Williams about the soup and stuff: what was it like? He put his hands in his pockets and thought for a while and then said, 'It's a bit like that story old Thomas was reading to us. About Oliver Twist and his butties, only usually there's none left for you to ask for more.'

We were sitting on a log of wood on the lower slope of the hill just outside the village. Two miners – timbermen – had sharpened up their axes and had felled two of the tallest trees in a small ash copse. For firewood, they said, but it was really to sooth the itch in their hands, aching to grip the shaft of an axe again. We picked up the chips of white wood that still lay around and threw them idly into the river a few yards below, and then we watched them float gently down until they were lost in a swirl of water as the stream hurried between two big rocks. Since the pits were idle the river had become as clear as a mountain stream. Even in its deepest part, the stones with their red-iron tinge could easily be seen. During the summer holidays we had bathed in it and sunned ourselves on the rocks. The water became so clear that the trout came down again from the upper reaches. A fisherman gave us a small fish one afternoon. We cooked it over a wood fire and ate it with potatoes, roasted in the embers. The colliers dammed up the stream at one part with big stones and turf and made a pond deep enough for diving. In this pond we learned to swim.

Even after it had become too cold to bathe we still haunted the river and watched it change to its melancholy autumn face, with dead leaves swirling round the deserted pool. The river just then was like the valley during the strike and the stop-days which followed: no flow, nor warmth, with decay floating about on its surface.

Ginger tossed a piece of bark into the water and said, 'When the strike's over, I'll be going into the pit. The old gent says so.'

'Do you want to go down?'

He threw another piece of the felled tree into the water before answering, 'I'll have a go at it. I'm tired of school and, besides, I'll be able to go to the pictures every Friday night.'

'But I thought you wanted to go to sea?'

'Ay, but I'll have to stay home for a bit to help them catch up after the strike. The old gent will be lucky if he gets back to work when it's all over – he's on the Strike Committee. I shan't want to stay in school, anyhow.'

That evening I called for him on the way down from taking a parcel to one of the top houses. He was having tea. I waited outside, but his mother called me in and I sat on the sofa while they finished their tea – Ginger, his mother and the baby, and two of his little brothers.

I was uncomfortable on the sofa. I didn't want to be there while they were having tea. They had just started.

There was a bowl of beetroot in the centre of the table, nothing else. Ginger and his brothers had two pieces of bread and dripping for their meal. Their mother cut the bread and placed the pieces on their plates. There was only one piece on hers. She was a stoutish woman with light hair and she sat at the table casually, as though it were somewhere where you sat down out of habit and not for any particular purpose. She placed the baby on her knee and half-turned towards me and said, 'We can't ask you to have anything, *bach*, we're on strike.'

One of Ginger's brothers – the one who'd cut his head when he fell off the school wall – looked at his mother. He had cleared his plate, but he couldn't catch his mother's eye for some time as she was sitting sideways to the table, but I could see that she knew what he wanted. At last he said quietly, ignoring the looks of the others, 'Mam, Mam, can I have another piece?'

She didn't turn round, but answered him sharply, 'No more now. A piece each for supper.' But I could see by her face that she wasn't angry, only tired and a bit afraid.

Ginger finished and nodded towards the door. As we went out his mother called out after him in a shrill voice, 'Glyn, Glyn!' I wondered who she was calling until I remembered Ginger's name. He went back and, after a while, came out, looking very angry.

'I got to call in Davies the Chapel first, to get a parcel.'

'It's not far,' I said, 'we'll soon get it over.'

But he still seemed displeased and I didn't find out why until later, when Mrs Davies handed him a brown bulging parcel at the top of the steps to their house and I saw him carry it down with a strange look on his face and his eyes shining. If I didn't know Ginger I'd have said that he was going to cry.

But the strike brought excitement too. Ginger said as we went to school one afternoon, 'There's going to be a big trial tomorrow morning. They're going to try a man for speaking the truth to the miners in Aberdare.'

Although it was strange that they were going to try a man for speaking the truth, this slipped to the back of my mind. What was more important: could we see this man; would there be any chance of us going to the trial? We stopped and went into the doorway of an old shed where we could talk without being overheard.

'I heard my father say the case is coming on at eleven o'clock tomorrow morning.'

'But we'll be in school.'

Ginger nodded. 'Ay, supposed to be. There's the trouble.'

After talking it over we decided that we could get away from school during the morning break, on the excuse of going home to fetch our library books which we'd forgotten.

That night there were many new faces in the village, and the groups of miners stood around till a much later hour. The policemen paraded in groups of four, and there were a lot more than usual. Ginger said they had come from Liverpool and were sleeping in the Long Room of the Pantcynon Hotel, with their truncheons all piled up ready on the table.

We saw them next morning. They marched down like soldiers, through the main streets where there was a big crowd and on to the Police Court. They made a big line round the Court, pressing the people back onto the pavements to keep the road clear. Ginger and I slipped in to the front of the crowd and found that Fatty Hughes was there before us. He had developed a sore throat so he couldn't go to school that morning. We asked him if anything had happened.

'Not yet,' he said expectantly, 'the bloke they're going to try hasn't come yet.' Then a secret look came over his face and he winked and pointed at the policeman nearest to us. We looked at him but could see nothing unusual. 'His sleeve, his sleeve,' Fatty whispered. We could see the end of a leather strap just under the sleeve of his overcoat. We glanced at one another and edged further from him into the crowd.

Half an hour later, a big police car came slowly through the lines of policemen. The crowd stirred, and there was shouting and cheering which died down as soon as the car stopped. Four big policemen and a short, round man with glasses got out of the car. The round man was smiling and, as the four policemen marched him quickly to the court, the crowd started to cheer again. He raised his hand in salute and they surged forward, and for a moment it looked as if the crowd would storm after him, into the courtroom where the police had quickly hustled him, but more police came running up with white faces, and the crowd hesitated, and then was gradually pushed back onto the pavement again. We waited for a long time outside the courtroom but nothing happened, except when Jack Ragtime and a few more miners started poking fun at a big sergeant who had a fat neck that bulged over his collar. It went redder and redder as they asked him if he had ever been on strike, and whether he'd had three rashers of bacon for breakfast that morning, or four.

It was late that night, long after we had gone to bed, that the trouble started, when they escorted the round man down to the station to take him to Cardiff Gaol, ready for the Assizes. We saw next morning the broken windows and the stones scattered about the road.

There were three of us at the washing. Outside the back of the house was a wooden bench, with two big wooden tubs and a tin bath alongside. Arthur was given the whites, I had the flannels, while Nipper had the napkins. On Monday, everything in the house had to wait on the washing. By the end of the day there were two lines full and an overflow on the wooden railings. If it rained, the house was not a place to live in, on that day. Since the strike, Mother and Dinah had been doing all the washing themselves. Mrs Roberts, who used to come on Mondays and tell us all about her husband who came home 'primed up' on a Saturday night – all over her shoulder as she hustled the clothes about, left for London where she was going to live with a married daughter. So Mother decided to do the job herself and save expense. It was a mountainous job – she and Dinah worked like slaves on Mondays.

But we had a long weekend from school, and Dinah had egged on Arthur and me to have a try at the washing. She said it would be good fun and our hands would be as white as milk when we'd finished, and she promised that if we finished the washing we shouldn't have anything more to do that day; if we worked, the whole wash could be finished by dinnertime. Nipper came in of his own accord. After he had listened to Dinah persuading us, he thought he'd be missing something if he stayed out. We placed the long duck-board on the stone flags alongside the bench, put on canvas aprons and started. Mother and Dinah stood in the doorway laughing and making encouraging remarks for the send off.

We bent our backs over the washing-boards and started to scrub merrily. The swish of the clothes as we drew them over the ribbed board, and the splash as they went into the water, made a more or less regular rhythm that kept us going for five minutes. Then we threw a napkin and two handkerchiefs into the bath on the floor.

Nipper looked critically at his hands. 'I believe it does make your hands clean. Look at mine!'

'Ay, they'll be like girls' hands before we finished. What about some more hot water?'

I went into the scullery which was clouded with steam and ladled out a bucketful of boiling water from the copper.

'And some more soap!'

I took a bar of soap from the shelf and cut it into three equal pieces. We plastered it on the washing-board, making sure that we should not fail through lack of soap.

Dinah came out and cast a quick eye over the tubs. She saw the extra soap. 'Where did you get all that soap from? Soap alone won't get them clean. You've got to use elbow-grease. Let me show you.' She took a napkin out of Nipper's bath and attacked it as though she were trying to wear it out on the washing-board. Then she wrung it out deftly and threw it into the bath on the floor. She took one of Arthur's handkerchiefs and held it up. 'Not too bad! Of course the whites will have to be boiled later on.'

Nipper and I realized we had chosen the wrong tub, because any of Arthur's failures had a good chance of being righted in the boil. Yet he had to reach the highest standard.

I was sweating over a flannel shirt. The cuffs were surely a different colour from the rest of the shirt – scrubbing seemed to make little difference to them. I took it out of the water and examined the neckband. 'Whose shirt is this?'

Arthur looked at it, 'It's not mine. Too small for me.'

Nipper said, 'It's mine,' though not very possessively.

'Perhaps you'd like to have a try at washing it. Have you been cleaning your boots with the cuffs?'

'Oh, throw it in, I can wear it with my sleeves tucked up. Throw it in!'

We scrubbed silently for another ten minutes, then our pace began to slacken. The sweat was beginning to collect on our faces yet we had hardly made an impression on the pile of clothes beside the bench.

I called to Dinah who was inside the scullery, 'It's an extra big wash this week, Dinah?'

'Extra big? Go on with you. I've not been upstairs to collect the rest of it yet.'

Arthur said, 'At this rate we'll be here till next Monday. We'll have to quicken it up.'

We scrubbed again, giving less time to each garment, and the pile began to diminish. We sat down on the edge of the bench to rest. Arthur saw me looking critically at the clothes we had washed. 'There's one thing: they'll be cleaner after the boil. The sun makes 'em whiter too.'

Just after we started another burst, the upstairs window opened and out came a cascade of soiled linen, dropping neatly on top of us. Dinah called out, 'That's some of it,' and before we had recovered from the setback, Mother came out with another armful from the living-room.

'That's the lot, Ma,' Dinah called, 'I can't find any more.'

Arthur looked up. 'What about a few blankets? We may as well make a wash of it. And how about the curtains?'

Dinah closed the window. 'Get on with it, my lad. We'll soon find you more when you've finished that.'

Our backs ached and our knuckles were sore. We wiped our hands, and Arthur went to get some cake from the larder. As we ate the cake Nipper said, 'I've had enough. My hands are clean enough.'

'Clean? Look at mine. There's a blister coming up in that knuckle. What a job!'

Arthur had an idea and got up quickly from his seat. 'What about the dolly? That will help.'

'Where is it?'

We soon found the dolly – a handle with a big boss of wood at the end of it for pounding the dirt out of the clothes. We lifted the tub of flannels onto the floor, thrust in the dolly, and pounded them with new energy. But at first there was a little argument about the way of using the dolly. I was in favour of using it like a hammer, beating it down on the clothes with all the weight of the shoulders behind it – all the dirt would be battered out, that way. Arthur's way was more scientific. He had seen Mrs Roberts hustling the clothes with the dolly. She used sharp staccato prods with a quick turn of the wrist at the end of each prod, so that the clothes were seized and twisted mercilessly between the legs of the dolly. Each of us had a turn, keeping strictly to his own method, while Nipper dabbled in both. The gross pile beside the tub became much smaller, but dollying was too drastic for the whites and once more we had to go back to the washing-boards. The return was hard, and at this point we very nearly took off our aprons. But Mother came out and congratulated us on our washing.

'Well, you've nearly finished it. Just this tubful and those old trousers of David's. You're making a better job of it than old Mrs Roberts.' She took a garment and rubbed it out over the board to encourage us.

With another half-hour's spurt, we got to the last garment: Nipper's trousers. They were pretty dirty. Arthur asked him, 'What colour's your trousers, Nipper, dark black or ebony?'

We threw them into the tub and harried them with the dolly. But they still kept most of the dirt. Then we slapped them on the stone flags and scrubbed them with a stout cane sweeping-brush. They began to show signs of the original colour after this. Nipper took them up and looked at them doubtfully. 'How about the buttons? They look squashed.'

Arthur said, 'There's plenty of new buttons in the house. You always reckon to lose a few buttons if you send things to the laundry.'

When we had finished the trousers, we went through the garments sorting them out ready to hang on the line. Dinah said, 'Don't go putting up bad washing on the line. You've got a reputation to keep up. Look at these napkins – there's no grain at all in them.'

We decided that the napkins had better not go on the line. 'Put 'em on the railings,' Nipper suggested. But they wouldn't do, even for the railings.

'You have a try at washing 'em. They won't come any cleaner.'

We tried them with the dolly and with the stiff broom and found that Nipper was right. Arthur said, 'It'll come out in the boil.'

We boiled the napkins but still they looked no different. We were getting impatient to finish. I said recklessly, 'Dip the blue-bag in with them. That will help.'

We experimented with the blue. Nipper said, 'But you've made them worse. Now what are we going to do?'

We had been successful so far and we were not going to be beaten by a few napkins so, to improve them, to bring out the whiteness which was sure to be there after all the washing they'd had, we decided to give them the smallest splashing of starch. Even then they didn't look very promising as they drooped over the railings, but we persuaded ourselves that, by some miracle of wind and weather, the next morning would see their whiteness.

It did. The clothes were left out all night, since it hadn't been drying weather during the day. Nipper went out, as soon as he got downstairs, to see our handiwork. He came in to breakfast saying, 'The clothes are looking fine. They're quite dry, but the ones on the railings are frozen.'

'Frozen?' Dinah said, 'There couldn't have been a frost

last night. And how aren't the others frozen as well?'

She hurried out the back and whisked one of the napkins off the railings, peered at it and rubbed it briskly between the knuckles of both hands. Then she looked at the three of us – we'd followed her out apprehensively. She was trying to be scornful but she couldn't keep a straight face, and as she bent the napkin into a fold she burst out laughing, 'Poor baby!' and she asked me, 'Did you do this on purpose?'

'Well,' we said, 'you wanted a good grain on the napkins.'

And Arthur added seriously, 'Look at them. There's lovely and white they are. If there really had been a frost they couldn't be whiter.'

I had more work to do in the evenings and on weekends. I was able to haul sacks of meal and corn from the goods station, and sometimes to serve in the shop. I was serving when the gypsies came.

Father got on well with the gypsies. They came to the village two or three times a year and camped on a narrow strip of ground just under the big rock that jutted out from the mountain. They came to the shop in a drove this Saturday afternoon, with baskets and babies in arms and a small girl holding her mother's skirt. Although there were only three women, with their babies and baskets they filled the shop. They came in silently and placed the baskets down on the floor. Two of the women nursed babies in the folds of their shawls. The third – a much older woman – carried two baskets. She was a big woman and her cheekbones were high and her creased skin was like yellow parchment. One of the mothers was beautiful, with black glistening hair and full, red lips. Her back was very straight and she held her head high, as though she carried an invisible pitcher. She wore thick gold earrings. The second mother – a thin woman with hollow cheeks and a broad mouth showing widely-spaced teeth – set the little girl to sit down on her basket, which was still half full of clothes pegs.

The big woman looked around the shelves and the counter without showing much interest, as though there was little in the shop to make the money burn in her pocket. A thin cry came from the dark Queen's baby, and she undid her dress and gave it the breast with the same dignity she had shown when she first entered and looked around the shop.

They waited silently until Father had finished with a regular customer. They stood by the provision counter near the bacon and cheese. Father moved over towards them and the bargaining started. The big woman said abruptly without greeting, 'Some pegs left, *mistah*, only a few.' Her voice was hard and better made for threats than persuasion. Father knew the moves and wasn't to be hurried.

'Well, we've not seen you for a long time.' He rearranged the pieces of bacon on the counter as he spoke.

'Near a year now. We've been up in England. Will you have the pegs, *mistah*?'

'Where are you camping?'

'Same place. Have a look at the pegs, sir.' She glanced down at the little girl and, with a small movement of her hand, waved her aside. The girl got up and the big woman pointed to the bundles of pegs, made from ash wood and thin strips of tin for binding. The pegs were threaded on long strips of bark or osier.

Father glanced, a bare glance over the counter. 'But I've got a box full of pegs here.'

'Just a few. Don't let us take them home. Only ninepence.' Her voice became softer. 'Just a few coppers, sir.'

Father handed over the money out of the till. 'You'd sell coal to the colliers.'

The big woman shrugged her shoulders and kept the coins in her hand, while the little girl, without waiting to be told, gathered up the pegs and placed them on the counter. 'Got any bacon, *mistah*?'

Father pointed with a wave of the hand to the counter, 'There we are.' But he knew what she meant, and brought out some odd pieces – ham-bones and ends – from behind a pile of tin stuff.

She bargained for them, trying to get as many pieces as she could for sixpence. Father was slow to close the bargaining, merely for the sport of it, and to avoid the appearance of being overridden, because he really wanted to get rid of the accumulation of scrap ends. The gypsy woman knew this and kept on the attack,

'A piece more, sir. Just another piece, special for my man.'

Father put another piece on the pile and flicked the counter with his apron. 'There, you've got them all. You can have boiled bacon for a week.'

The thin-faced mother nodded her head towards the cheese, but the big woman still did the talking – the other was content to watch her practised bargaining. She cajoled

143

all the small pieces of cheese onto the counter and at last handed over the threepence, not forgetting to tell Father that he was really having his money back.

Father asked her, 'And how much will I get for your pegs?'

'Get as much as you can, *mistah*. They're good pegs – all made by hand, and they'll bring the women luck.'

Father caught my eye and whispered to me, 'Some broken biscuits in a bag,' nodding towards the little girl. She became alive as I filled the paper bag.

The big woman nodded to Father, 'You'll live a long time, sir, and your wife will bring you many children.'

Father pretended to smooth his moustache as he said, 'Thank you. You are very kind.' I too saw the joke, and had so far lived down the family as to be able to laugh at it.

The man in the Band of Hope stood for an hour in front of the purple banner, and said that life was like a train journey: sometimes you went slow, and sometimes you went fast; sometimes you were too cold, and sometimes you were too hot; and sometimes you went through a plain, and sometimes you found yourself going up an incline. Wherever you went, you would always see different scenes and changes, if you didn't fall asleep. He warned us against the danger of falling asleep. But supposing you had gone through a long tunnel, so long that it seemed as if the train would never come out, what a delight it was to wake and see the country all green and fresh after the darkness of the tunnel.

I remembered the man's lecture very well, though he said a lot that I couldn't understand, about missing the train altogether and getting on the wrong train and not paying the right fare. He was a bit terrifying when he said this. He was a whiskered man with tufts of hair growing out of his ears. He pointed at the front row of the Band of Hope and asked us in a loud voice, 'Are you sure you are paying the conductor the right fare?' We all sat up at this fierce question, trying to look as honest and as innocent as we could. 'Make sure, boys and girls, that you pay the conductor the right fare!'

Some said he was a missionary, but others said he had only been to America. For a long time after the whiskered man's visit to the Band of Hope, I thought of his lecture. Life is like a journey. What a dull journey at times. How exciting at others. But always changes.

When Dinah bought herself a new costume and a new hat, and John Prosser began to come to the house more often, and when they used to talk together in the front room, we guessed they were going to get married. If Dinah was going to leave home, it was a change we were not going to like. I was afraid to ask her if it was true, because it was so hard to think of living here without her. Who would get us to bed if she went? Who would look behind our ears? Who would get our suppers? And who would get us out of scrapes? Dinah must have known what was in our minds, because when I grumbled at doing a job she told me, 'You think yourself hard-pressed now. But you wait a bit, my lad.'

She hinted that there would be more clothes washing and more lighting of fires. She was only fooling, since it came out later that, although she was getting married, she was not leaving home, at least not straight away. John

Prosser was coming to stay with us until they could get a house. Arthur and I were going to shift our bed into the boxroom where all the trunks and the chest for the linen were kept.

We looked forward to the wedding. It would be exciting having John Prosser to stay with us; it would be like having another brother. And the wedding itself would be something. Dinah would probably get married in the chapel next door, and our Tom would be best man, and after it was all over he'd come out on the steps and throw out a handful of pennies, with a sixpenny piece or two thrown in, so that we could scramble for them. There would be jelly and blancmange, and we'd all be in our best clothes with our hair smoothed down with vaseline, and a white flower in our buttonholes. And, if we were lucky, there'd be a whole day off from school.

Castles. High Castles in the air! For, when the arrangements were made, we found that Dinah wasn't going to be married in the chapel. She wanted a quiet wedding, and they were going to be married in a registry. They weren't going on a honeymoon, not yet – John Prosser couldn't be spared from work, and it wasn't safe to spare himself. If he did, the job wouldn't be there when he came back. They would have a holiday later in the year. Most likely there'd be a holiday in any case, when the pits went on short time.

On the morning of the wedding we were up very early. John Prosser had stayed with us the night before. He and Dinah with our Tom were going to catch the first train down the valley. They were going to be married in the registry office in Pontycyw, and afterwards they were all going on to Cardiff to have dinner at an hotel. Then they were coming back to the house in the evening, and we were going to have a real family supper. We were not going to the wedding, but we were going to send them to the station.

Nipper was the first awake that morning. He shook me and said, 'This is the day Dinah is going to get married.' He put his head out through the window. 'Is it going to be a fine day? Will they be lucky?'

A fine early-morning mist rose up from the river, covering the grass of the valley. The top of the hills stood out sharply against the sky. 'Yes, it's going to be fine. But I thought a wet day was lucky for a wedding?'

Arthur came in. 'Are you going to put your best clothes on?'

'Yes.'

'But it's not as if we're going to the wedding.'

'Never mind, we're the escort.'

The others were early up, and Mother was at the top of the table pouring out tea. Father was chatting with John Prosser and Tom, while Dinah was sitting holding the baby, with a white cloth covering her skirt. The tea cosy with the worked-in design was over the teapot, showing that it was a very special occasion.

Tom said to John Prosser as he passed the toast, 'Come on now, John, eat up. It's your last breakfast as a single man.'

Mother said, 'Why do you say that now? You'll frighten him.'

'Frighten me, that's quite true, Ma. Anybody would think I was going to be hanged, not married.' He looked at Dinah with a pretence of sternness.

147

She winked at him and said to Tom, 'Your turn will come – don't be so cocksure. You may be at your own wedding before you've worn that suit of clothes out.'

Tom shook his head and said, 'This is a new suit and it will have to last a long time. Ten years, maybe.'

'You'll be a family man by then.'

'Whose family? No, I was born for better things.'

After Father had asked Tom whether he'd got all the papers, and whether he knew the times of the trains, and after the couple had shaken hands with Mother and Father, we set out. Dinah looked fine and strange in her dark costume. We crowded round her. Nipper on one side, and Arthur and I on the other, so that John Prosser had to walk with Tom, in front. He pretended to be annoyed, saying it was a poor thing if a chap couldn't walk his girl to their own wedding.

At the station, an old woman came across the platform towards us. She had a shawl around her black coat, and carried a big basket. She put it down and said to Dinah, in a thin voice, 'Getting married you are, Rachel?' She kissed Dinah on the cheek. 'Good luck, my gel. I remember you when you were a little baby and used to nurse you in these very arms.'

Dinah said simply, 'Thank you, Mrs Gwyther.'

John Prosser asked her, 'How long ago was that, Mother? I'm not so sure whether she's been telling me her right age.'

The old woman laughed shrewdly and raised her hands. 'Well, you're slow, *bychan*. Haven't you seen the birth certificate?' John Prosser slapped his thigh and the old woman said, 'Look after her, my boy, and she'll make a

148

good wife to you.'

'But it's me she's going to look after, Mrs Gwyther. That's why I'm marrying her.'

The old woman shrugged her shoulders, laughing, and as the train came in she picked up her basket calling out 'Good luck', as she moved down the platform.

When they were in the train, John Prosser leaned out through the window and, as he talked to us, he slipped a half-crown into my hand and whispered, 'Instead of the pennies!'

Just before the train moved off, Dinah came to the window too and said lightly, 'We'll be back soon. Don't forget to chop the sticks, will you?'

Nipper made a face at her, but as the train moved off we shouted together, 'We'll be waiting for you.'

We walked home, and I felt the chill of the early morning and noticed the drab, dusty lane leading from the station, with tins and soiled paper lying at the front of the railings. It would be a long day until the evening, when they would return. What were we to do until then? We would have to change back into our everyday clothes. It was hard to have a holiday mood damped by changing into a pair of corduroy breeches. It was hard to be cheerful, all dressed up in your best clothes so early in the morning with no special place to go. My fingers closed round the half-crown which lay, for the moment, forgotten in my pocket. Here, anyway, was solid comfort. The rest of the way home was taken up in sharing out the half-crown and making plans for spending it.

The party came home very soon after I had milked the

cow – Tom had shown us how it was done, and it was a thing now to boast about. Dinah didn't look any different for being married, nor did John Prosser. There was a big supper laid on the table with the best white cloth, all ready waiting for them. Father had changed, and waxed his moustache as he sometimes did, and sat at the head of the table, ready to carve. Mother, who looked younger with her hair frizzed up in small curls and wearing a white lace collar, served us all with supper before Dinah could get her to sit down.

There was plenty of laughing, and John and our Tom told about the wedding, and how they had to get another witness – an old man from an office downstairs – who looked a bit fed up about it, although he was getting one-and-sixpence for just signing his name – more suitable for standing-in at a funeral, than a wedding. Then, at the end of the supper, Father got up and went to the cupboard and got out a bottle and put it on the table. I'd often caught a glimpse of this bottle in Father's cupboard, which he always kept locked. It was a round bottle, not very big, with a very long neck, and it was covered with straw plaited very closely together, and the cork was sealed with gilt. Father placed it on the table and turned to John Prosser. 'Rachel knows what it is, John. It's a bottle of champagne. Her uncle brought it back from France many more years than I'd like to tell and I've been keeping it in the cupboard for this occasion.'

Arthur said to me knowingly, 'It's champagne. You hear it pop and watch the bubbles when it's opened.'

'There's enough for a taste all round.'

We all watched Father use the corkscrew and waited for the pop, but it didn't come, and as he poured out the wine it was flat in the glasses.

'I know what's up,' said Arthur, 'the cork has perished. It's got dry. You should have kept the bottle standing up on its head, Pa, to keep the cork moist,'

'Perhaps so,' Father said, smiling, 'there are no bubbles. But it doesn't matter, we'd not get drunk on it even if there were.'

He poured out a sip for everyone, and we drank the couple's health and luck, and no one was disappointed because there were no bubbles. Mother even turned it into a good omen.

We were having breakfast when my Father said, 'There's an order in for Penywaun. I want you to take the goods up in the cart. David will go with you.'

I couldn't eat any more after this. Penywaun was a farm away up on the hog's-back of the hill, about four miles out of the village. It was a tricky journey with a horse and cart; narrow mountain roads and a hill as steep as your forehead. This was the first time I was to make the journey under my own charge. I'd been driving the horse for some time, but I'd never been allowed to deliver goods up to the farm. It was a good feeling to think: now you can take care of the horse, like a man. For a journey to Penywaun was not an easy thing, with a two hundredweight sack of barley meal and a couple of hundredweight of maize and a lot of heavy goods besides. Father said, 'Eat your porridge now. Your wrists are as thin as sticks.'

As soon as breakfast was over, I went to look for David. He was still upstairs playing on the bed with a kitten. 'Get up, Nipper, quick. We're going up to Penywaun today. Just you and me. Hurry up.'

He was out of bed like a hare out of a hedge. I helped him to find his socks. There was a lot to be done – we were to start at two o'clock. It would take us an hour and a half to get to the farm. We were to stay to tea and be back before dark. Mrs Thomas was a good friend. We couldn't come away without tea, even if we told her 'no' a hundred times.

First we set to work on·the horse. Dick was sleek and looked well when he was groomed. We used the curry-comb on him, and then we brushed him down, making his mane shine like the hair of a girl. He looked like a show horse, and Father came out and praised us for the change in him. Nipper wanted to plait his mane and his tail with straw and a ribbon, but we thought it would look too gay and showy for a business horse. We put him back in the stable and gave him his fodder.

Nipper said, 'Put a bit extra in – some oats. He'll go faster.'

I put in two extra scoopfuls to make sure the horse wouldn't fail. Besides, it was a day out for him, too.

'He's going to have a pull up that mountain,' I said to Father as we loaded up.

'You lead him until you get on top. Take him slow, and tack from side to side of the road when you get to the bad bit by the Elbow. David can walk up the short cut through the fern. Have you got everything?'

I asked hopefully, 'Shall we take the lamps?'

'No, you won't need the lamps. Set out not later than

half-past six and you'll be back before dark.'

Then, at last, we started. As I took up the reins and clicked my tongue for the horse to move, I felt we were starting on a great journey.

We made our way very sedately down the street towards the mountain road. Neither Nipper nor I would have changed places with a king in his chariot. We were glad that there were people in the street. We wanted everybody to see us going about a man's important business.

When we got out of the village and the excitement of setting out fell away, I became conscious of my job, and started to run over in my mind all the things we had to do: tack from side to side; keep his head up if he starts slipping; go to the back door of the farm, not to the front; and don't forget to say thank you for the tea. I winked at Nipper, and he asked me if he could drive.

'When we get to the top.' I noticed his trousers. 'Aren't those your best?'

He shook his head. 'I've finished wearing them for best. I'm having a new pair. Don't like these. I'm going to do some sliding, to wear them out.'

We got to the foot of the hill and I sent Nipper up by the path through the bracken, while I led the horse round the road. We got up without much trouble and, at the top, Nipper was sitting on a boundary stone, tossing pebbles at a rock on the opposite side of the road. The worst part of the climb was over now. The rest was a gradual ascent over undulating moorland to the farm. But, before starting again, we turned back to look at the valley and the village hung up on its end, below.

'There's our house,' Nipper pointed excitedly, 'and there's the Travellers Rest.'

It was a bright soft day in late summer. A motor car crept slowly along the road down in the valley, and puffs of steam from an engine shunting in a siding dissolved into the air somewhere below us. A little way off, on the top of the hill, a lark rose out of the bracken and made a ladder out of its song. We sat down on a grass mound at the side of the road. I was proud that we had come so far, and I got up and patted the horse. He was resting with slack traces and his flanks rose and fell evenly. He had worked well. But Nipper got up into the cart. He was eager to be off and he was keeping me to my promise. 'You said I could drive when we reached the top.'

'All right. Hold the reins slack then.' He stood up proudly in the cart and clicked his tongue, and the horse bent his head once more.

Higher up, the road burrowed into the side of the hill and, on each side, was bounded by hedges of hawthorn and bramble with here and there a stretch of dry walling. There was nothing more exciting than a cow that thrust its head through a gap in the hedge – a catcall from Nipper sent it careering in an ungainly gallop over the fields.

We reached a lane that branched off from the road and became quickly lost in a copse of hazels. Nipper asked, 'Where does it go to?'

'Ty Coch. Ty's a big farm. The farmer's wife is always in her best clothes; her face is red and shiny. They say she takes a bottle of whiskey to bed with her.'

I had been over this road with Tom many times and

knew every turn in it. We came to a short hill and, after we had reached the top, we saw a group of white farm buildings, built just off the road, in the mother rock of the hill.

'That's Garth Fach, where the fairies are supposed to have gone to take the baby. The old woman saved it by putting a pair of iron tongs across the cradle.'

Nipper looked at me with a sort of accusing wonder, 'You don't believe in fairies, do you?' He was ready to have a big laugh at the fairies.

'Well, no,' I said, pretending to weigh up the matter of fairies very carefully, 'I don't believe that there are any now, but it makes the place different if you think there were once fairies in it.'

He was a bit puzzled by this, and said with vigour, 'I don't believe in them. It's all tommy-rot, like Santa Claus. Nobody's ever seen a fairy, unless it's chaps like old Benny Malt when they're tipsy.'

I shrugged my shoulders and had to admit that Nipper wasn't 'buying' the fairies.

Presently, the road dipped and showed a wooded hollow with the ruins of an old farmhouse, and above it a stream clinging precariously to the hillside. I said casually as I jumped out to lead the horse on the descent, 'That's Cwm Heldeg.'

Nipper seemed more interested – here was something to look at. It was one of those brooding hollows shut in by the full breast of the hills, and keeping some of its remoteness even in the brightest sunlight.

'Cwm Helen Deg; the Vale of Fair Helen. They say there's a story about the hollow and the farmhouse.'

'Who was she?' Nipper asked, 'Tell me about her. Did she live in the old farmhouse?'

I took the horse's bridle and said vaguely, 'I've heard the story, but I can't remember it.'

I was sorry to disappoint him. He was staring at the ruins of the old house, and even after we'd passed he still looked back. Then he said suddenly, 'You don't know the story. Well, can't you make one up about her?'

I laughed. 'And you wouldn't believe in the fairies!'

'But she was real; she wasn't a fairy. Else they wouldn't have named the place after her. I'd like to know the story. Make up a story about her!'

'I'll try,' I said aloud. Then, realizing I'd never made up a story before I added, 'By Christmas perhaps.'

We had reached the uncultivated moor, and the road had now lost its metalled surface and ran on the tough, close-napped turf of the hills, with the bedrock breaking through in patches. We went along slowly. Nipper jumped down from the cart and walked alongside, making sallies off the track to look for whinberries that grew in small turf mounds over the moor. I got into the cart and had a wide view of the moor, which was all covered with bracken and soft mossy patches, except for a small group of weather-bitten beeches lining the track just in front of us. I began to sing, and Nipper shouted, 'You're frightening the crows,' and he pointed to two birds rising heavily off the beeches.

We left the moor and passed through a gate into a lane running between two rough-pastured fields, and about half a mile farther along we reached the farm. It was protected on its northern side by a half-circle of fir trees. Nipper

156

opened the gate and we passed into the farmyard, while two sheepdogs made the buildings echo with a hollow show of hostility. A woman's voice shouted to them shrilly, but they still kept on barking. Then Mrs Thomas herself came out of the house and down the steps into the yard. She shouted again, and after a few isolated barks they quietened down and accepted us with a great tail-wagging and licking of hands. She called out, 'You've come up all right then, boys. Put the goods on the stone slab in the dairy. Dafydd will give you a hand with the sack stuff.' She glanced quickly at the horse, 'He's had a pull!'

She had a red face, with greyish-black hair drawn tightly over her head. Around her waist was a grey flannel apron. Although her voice was sharp, we had a feeling that whatever time we called we had been expected and that everything was ready for us. She beckoned to an old cow-man who was watching from one of the doors of the out-houses, and she called out in Welsh as he approached. 'Give the boys a hand, Dafydd, and put the pony in one of the bottom stalls.' She hustled up the steps, driving away two chickens that were patrolling around the dairy.

The old man came slowly across the yard. His hands were in his pockets, and he grinned at us knowingly. 'Pony's got bit of a sweat on.' His face was deep with wrinkles and creased up like a washing-board when he laughed. He had been at the farm for nearly twenty years and rarely went beyond it. 'How is your father keeping?' he asked. He was as simple as an animal and even a boy could see through his guile – he knew that there would be a small packet of twist-tobacco for him. He watched me taking it out of my pocket, accepted it quickly, winked, and placed it carefully in the pocket of his old moleskin waistcoat. 'The sacks we'll take into the loft over the big cowshed.'

We were excited and felt that we were on an adventure. Nipper whispered to me, 'Ask him if we can have a ride on that horse we saw grazing down in the meadow.'

The old boy showed us where we were to take the sacks. We didn't want his help – he was too stiff and slow – so we told him we could manage. There was a pulley to lift the sacks to the loft and it wouldn't be work for us to haul them up. The old boy went to give Dick a handful of hay and, after we had finished with the sack stuff, I hauled Nipper up to the loft with the pulley, making a loop of the rope for him to rest his foot.

We went to find Dafydd. He knew the right time to go in for tea – he'd been going for so long. He was down in the cowshed – we heard him from the yard. We thought there was someone in there with him, but it was only an old, sad cow he was talking to. He had just finished drenching her and there was a heavy smell of linseed oil about the stall. He still had the drenching horn in his hand. We went inside and he crooked his arm across the cow's back and started to chat about the Valleys, asking us about a certain man named Ianto. As Ianto had been dead for longer than we could remember, we couldn't help him. He'd asked my father many times before about this Ianto, but he could never realize that he was dead. Ianto was a rough-and-tumble in the village, and used to fight bare-fist on the mountainside. The old man had once won a bet on him, and perhaps he thought that Ianto was more than mortal man and would never admit that even death had beaten him. He said, 'Your father knows Ianto; you ask him to show you Ianto. He's the finest boxer in the Three Valleys. He would fight with the devil, would Ianto.'

The old cow kept looking round at him reproachfully, either to shame him for his words, or to remind him that he was a weight on her sick and unwilling back. But just when we'd had enough of listening to Dafydd and watching his light-blue eyes dancing under his shaggy eyebrows, he gave the old cow a slap on her back and said, 'Get over, *fuwch*. It's time for tea.' He went up the steps to the kitchen door – outside there was a bowl of water and a clean piece of canvas towelling to dry our hands. Dafydd dipped his hands in the bowl and tried to smooth down a grey tuft of stiff hair that stood up on his forehead. After we'd washed our hands, Nipper and I looked at our boots, but when we saw the old boy step into the kitchen with his boots covered with mud we went straight in after him.

The kitchen was big, with one small window and a low ceiling. As we entered we could see nothing except the fire and the two dogs lying before it. But we could hear Mrs Thomas saying, 'Come you in, boys, it's all ready.'

We found our way to the table and gradually began to make out the details of the room and the other people who were in it. The table was long and there was room enough for a dozen people to sit down together. Alongside the table there were sides of bacon hanging by big hooks from the oak beam. Dafydd was sitting at the end of a long settle and he had already started his tea. Mrs Thomas was at the head of the table, and there was a girl just bringing in a plate of bread and butter to put on the table. There was a young farm-hand opposite Dafydd and, in the corner on the settee by the dresser, there was someone else. I couldn't see who it was because of the dark shadow, but I saw a patch of garment caught in a ray of sunlight and I knew it was a girl. Nipper and I sat down on the same long bench as Dafydd. William, the young farm-hand, was between us and the girl in the corner. Mrs Thomas was saying something but I only heard her dimly. I was puzzling about the girl in the corner: who was she? It wasn't one of the Thomas girls. They were away in Cardiff.

'Help yourself. Don't be afraid of it.'

I started back as Rosy, the serving girl, slipped a hot plate covered with toasted cheese in front of us. If only I could see her face!

Then Mrs Thomas said to the girl in the corner, 'They won't come down to tea. Come on you up to the table, Miss Edwards.'

I stopped eating and waited anxiously for the girl to come out of the shadows, because I had pictured her as fair as a fable and now I waited to see what was her beauty. The first thing I was conscious of as she moved into the light was a blazer of rich blue stripes undulating slightly over her breasts. She sat down opposite Nipper. He was eating, but when he looked up and saw her he stopped and she smiled quietly at his open-eyed gaze. I said to myself, 'I knew it. Something told me she would be lovely,' and the sight of the girl sent the day soaring above the flatness of other days. She smiled, but not specially in my direction, and I saw the smoothness of her skin with

160

her dark hair parted in the centre.

Mrs Thomas said, 'These are the Pritchard boys from the shop. They've brought a load up themselves. Miss Edwards is Davey Edwards our foreman's sister. You know Davey, don't you?'

Nipper and I both agreed vigorously.

'Miss Edwards is on holiday, the same as you.'

Nipper looked at her incredulously. She saw his words and smiled. 'No, not from school.'

I asked her boldly, 'What College are you at?' and she said, 'Cardiff,' as if it was quite a natural thing to be in a college. How distant it seemed, where the students wore gowns and strolled about the gardens.

But old Dafydd, who had been grinning at her ever since she came to the table, now heaved in like a bullock. 'I know Cardiff, Miss, like the back of my hand. My brother Wil was married in Splott. He had a wedding-cake as big as a church spire. I was down at the Royal Show too. There's a show for you.' He caught Mrs Thomas' frown and he sank back into his tea mumbling, 'That was a show, Miss.'

Rosy, the serving girl, sat opposite William, the farm-hand, and although he didn't raise his eyes, he was aware that she had sat down. She was round with a broad face and red hands; she was trying to catch William's attention but, like us all, he couldn't keep his eye off Miss Edwards. Rosy looked pointedly at him, ignoring the other girl except to pass the bread or the cake, which she did with great politeness.

Nipper was halfway through his plate of cheese, but he kept looking at the hunk of bread beside his plate and, at last, before I guessed what was in his mind and could tap his foot to stop him, he asked, 'Can I have some butter with my bread, please?'

Mrs Thomas looked stern and said firmly in the same tone as she told Rosy how much corn she was to give the chickens, 'We don't have butter with cheese at the farm. Your parents do spoil you, that's the trouble.'

In spite of her sharpness I could see that she was laughing quietly, and Miss Edwards too was smiling at Nipper. I was jealous of the look she was giving him. It was worth being refused butter to have a look like that.

While Mrs Thomas was joking with Nipper about the butter, Rosy and the farm-hand were tying glances over the table; she was trying to make him understand something, but he was pretending he didn't know what she meant.

Old Dafydd made another sally into the conversation. 'When I was a *crwtyn* of a boy, we never saw butter except on a Sunday and then it was spread so thin we had to hold the bread up to the light to see it.'

There was a silence after Dafydd spoke, and Mrs Thomas took hold of the conversation. 'Your brother and Mr Thomas are up with the men bringing in the oats. It's a big field just below the Common. You boys know it, no doubt?'

Nipper spoke excitedly, 'I saw them. They were stacking the oats in the corner of the field just where the wall meets the hedge.'

'That's right, my boy. You got some eyes in your head, I can see.' Mrs Thomas passed Nipper the plate of cake, as though to reward him for his sharpness.

One of the dogs got up from the fire. There was always

a fire even on the hottest days of summer. He strolled across the stone flags and lazily brushed against our legs. I stroked his smooth coat and he returned as lazily again to the mat, as much as to say, 'You two are all right; you can come again.'

Miss Edwards was talking to Nipper. 'Can you drive a horse?'

'Our horse is easy to drive, except sometimes he squints over to the left. But all you have to do is just to flap the rein on that side and he'll look round again to the front. He just wants to see what's coming up behind, but he can't because of the blinkers.' He was chatting to her while I was jealous of his ease and ashamed at my own dumbness.

'Could you take me for a drive in your cart?'

I didn't like the way she was playing with my brother. She didn't want to come for a ride really. I turned my head and pretended not to listen. I noticed Rosy was redder in the face. She had caught William looking with sheep's eyes at Miss Edwards and was kicking his foot under the table. I saw how he looked, and heard the crunch of his foot on the sand of the flagstones as he withdrew it, frowning at her angrily.

A moment later, Dafydd got up laboriously from his place at the table, drew his hand across his mouth and rolled out of the kitchen, saying that he was going to the cattle. William followed him after a while, ignoring Rosy who started to clear the dishes away noisily.

Mrs Thomas began to stir after the brief relaxation for the meal. 'You boys can stay as long as you like, only I expect you'll want to get home before dark. Rosy will collect some eggs for you to take back.' Then her purpose hovered about Miss Edwards. 'You can go up with the boys. That's an idea. You boys can take Miss Edwards up to the Common on your way back. You are going home that way, aren't you?'

Miss Edwards said, 'I'd like to very much,' and Nipper and I were lifted off the earth.

Nipper said, 'You can come in the cart and I'll show you how to drive.' He turned to me, 'I can drive, can't I?'

I nodded doubtfully, and tried to cover up my first reaction with a quick, 'Yes, certainly.' Already I had pictured myself driving while she looked on admiringly, as I persuaded Dick into a brisk trot.

We all went out with Rosy to collect the eggs, but we soon tired of raking the dusty barns and the hedgerows. I knew that Miss Edwards was bored, but I didn't want to leave the farm although she was coming with us part of the way. What could we do to keep her a little longer? I thought of the big meadow and asked her, 'Have you been to the front of the house?'

She came with us through the front garden, with its monkey tree that looked so out of place, and the grass growing right up to the front door that hadn't been opened for years. The meadow sloped gently away from the house, and was skirted at the bottom by a hedge that divided it from a smaller pasture beyond. In one corner there was a small drinking-pond with a cow-track leading down to it. The meadow had the light even green of a field that had given hay earlier in the year, and clung to the hillside like a well-cut garment. We went through the gate leading from the garden of the house, and stopped to look down and beyond into the Valleys – the Valleys themselves were only shadows cleaving the turbulence of the uplands. The more distant hills had a velvet covering of blue. The green patchwork of the fields below – each field of a different shade – vibrated in the sunlight.

I watched her secretly, hoping to read her thoughts as she looked at the scene, but her face was sad and I wondered where she found the sadness in a country that showed now at its kindest. Was the sadness inside her? But she said suddenly, 'Let's race down to the pond.' And before I had grasped the quick change, she had taken Nipper's arm on the one side and mine on the other, and we were racing down the slope in a wind-cutting rush, our feet noisily whipping the top of the thick grasses.

After the first surprise of the impulse, I became aware of her nearness; the smooth pressure of her arm and the clasp of her hand. I glanced sideways at her face. She was laughing and had given herself over completely to the race. I wanted to sing out. I looked at her again, at the glow of her skin in the sun, but she glanced at me from the corner of her eye and shouted, 'Come on. Run! Run! You're holding back.' And I laughed too and Nipper gave his shrill call and we got to the pond out of breath.

For a few moments we could not speak, and then we sat down on the turf mound of the hedge and started to talk like old friends. Then Nipper, who had been watching her intently, stood up and asked her with something of a challenge, 'Is your name Helen?'

She looked puzzled and turned to me, and when she saw

my confusion she said, 'Tell me, why Helen?'

I had to tell her of the ruined farm and of Cwm Heldeg, and she looked at Nipper and suddenly ruffled his hair. He got up and started to throw stones into the pond, and she and I talked about school; and she told me about the college.

As we climbed the slope again, I remembered that she was coming with us and I was eager to set off. She went into the house while we harnessed the horse. We went up to say goodbye to Mrs Thomas.

After a while, Mrs Thomas came out. She gave us the eggs and told us, 'Put them safe and watch they don't get scrambled.'

We said, 'Thank you for the tea,' and we'd enjoyed ourselves as much as a holiday, and she said, 'Come again before you grow up, and don't forget to drop Miss Edwards on the Common. Don't take her home with you.'

She had a red scarf around her neck when she returned and she looked different – during the short time she had been in the house she seemed to have become a stranger. The spell had broken. As she climbed into the cart, she handed me a camera and said, 'I'm going to take your photographs.' Then we were ready to go and Mrs Thomas and Rosy stood on the balcony and waved, while old Dafydd held the gate for us. I thought with a leap of excitement inside me: the day is not over yet; she's coming with us.

When we got into the lane, I handed Nipper the reins and he stood in the centre of the cart and coaxed the horse into a quick trot, so we had to cling onto the sides as the wheels bumped over stones on the road's uneven surface. We came to a sharp pull just before getting to the moor, or the 'Common' as Mrs Thomas called it, and she and I got out of the cart and walked.

The slanting rays of the sun filtered through the leaves of the high bushes and everything was covered with a delicate red-tinged light. Too soon, we reached the gate to the Common, and Nipper, who had got up before us, shouted that the harvesters were still in the field. When we climbed on the wall beside the gate, we could see them below outlined against the yellow oat-stubble. I asked her, 'You'll come with us as far as the beech trees? You can cut across to the field from there. That will be shorter.'

We got into the cart and once more bumped silently over the springy turf until we reached the trees. She said, 'This is a good spot for a snap.'

There wasn't any time to see if we were tidy or to wipe the mud off Dick's hoofs. We stood him against the trees and Nipper stayed in the cart, while I held Dick's head. She took two snaps of us. Then came the time for her to go. We both pointed out her way half a dozen times before she shook hands with us. We watched her walking through the bracken, but she turned suddenly and shouted, 'Where shall I send the snaps?'

I shouted back, 'The address on the cart.'

She came back and wrote the address in a small notebook, and was gone. We climbed into the cart because we could see her better as she skirted the other side of the hedge. The horse was impatient and started for home of his own accord. She turned and waved, then she went out of sight beyond the breast of the field. For a long time I could see the red of her scarf and the blackness of her hair.

Nipper said after a long silence, 'We'll get home before dark.'

'Easily.' I took up the slack reins and, as soon as we got to the good road, we came down like a round stone from the mountain. The steady rolling of the wheels was as soothing as a song. We unharnessed the horse just as it was getting dusk, and the rest of the day was like the small needless words at the end of a chapter.

A year passed, and I began climbing the steep hill out of boyhood. The previous summer was longer away than twelve months. With the new season had come a new life: the smooth reflecting pool was strangely rippled, and shadows blurred and obscured the old images, peopling the water with unfamiliar shapes. Occasionally, the old images would return, momentarily, but with a sharp-lined clearness. The girl we had met at the farm, in a light no summer day had seen; the stars as we walked home one night from Pontygwaith, each a merry eye in a broad heaven; the first warmth of spring on a hedge-bank; the ring of a horse's hoofs on a frost-hardened road.

At home, too, there had been changes. Dinah and John Prosser had gone to live on their own. They had found a house in a newly-built street at Brynllefrith and, although it was a second home for us, our own home had lost one of its letters. Tom was restless – more so since the strike, when business took a bad blow to the body. He was discontented and wanted to break away and set out on his own. Father, when he was writing a letter, would sometimes lay down his pen and stare out gravely through the window. Mother was the first up and last in bed, and work fell about her like the uneasy sound of a waterfall. Arthur had grown into my leggings, while I had Tom's, and Nipper was wearing Arthur's trousers. Gwyneth the baby could talk, and her hair was fairer than in a picture. We used to quarrel who was to carry her pick-a-back to the field. Mary and Betty, my two sisters who were staying with an aunt in the country, still belonged to the family though we only saw them at long intervals – little girls with straight black hair and straight manners.

We broke up school for the summer holidays – it was my last summer before leaving. The house, for me, had long begun to lose stature. My centre of interest had become displaced, and I saw the house from outside. The cosy evenings in the stable, the games in the living-room, the yarns in the loft, I saw with the cold eye of adolescence, belittling myself and everything that belonged to me. Outside was all that I had undervalued. Like a snail, I had been living in a small shell and thought that it was the world. Now the house and the family were dwarfed, painfully, by the new outgrowing. New covered lands opened out, and vague shapes paraded in pageantry before the mind's eye. There, nothing seemed certain. The girl at the farm was a symbol of a tract of undiscovered country, and her image came up with an intensity that increased with the growing distance in time. Although I could not remember how she looked, what she wore, what she said, she was more real even than when I had met her. She had never sent the photographs, as Nipper had often reminded me with regret, nor the snap of herself, as she had promised. Yet, that she had not done so threw a deeper light upon her. The girl at the farm! There was no need of a photograph. Even her name did not matter now. For me, she was as little in need of a name as the stars are in need of a guide-map, or the sunlight in need of the spectrum. Yes, the sunlight. It was chiefly by the sunlight that I could recapture that afternoon, which spread out and dwarfed all else, dividing me and pointing to the new life, disturbing and beautiful, that I was growing to.

Now, too, since Dinah had left, the family had lost its compactness. Nor was there the same order: we lost our Sunday collars and mislaid our boots; the hole in the sock spread, and there was no one to mend our shirts. Mother had too much to do. When all the small troubles mounted up and towered over us, we went up to visit Dinah in her house in Brynllefrith. Sometimes two of us together, or sometimes I went alone, taking a weighty burden of complaint for her to scatter to the winds.

Then, after a visit, I found that Dinah was going to have a baby. She was knitting something woolly when she told me in an off-hand way. But, instead of being puzzled and ashamed as I would have been a short while before, I now accepted small babies as one of the inescapable devices of providence, as apt to appear as unheralded, and sometimes as unaccountably, as a thunderbolt from the sky. Not that I didn't know the facts of life – I had gleaned those out of mud and out of print, but something had grown inside me, coating over the old painful conflict, helping me to accept even where I did not fully understand. And, when Dinah's baby was born, I felt no disturbing commotion within, but only a strange amusement, and even a tinge of interest in seeing whether a week-old baby was as much like the skinned rabbit as I remembered it to be.

It was about a week after the baby was born that I first saw it, on a Sunday evening. Nipper had gone up to spend the day in Dinah's, and I was to call in the evening. I was taking a visiting preacher to his home a couple of miles beyond Dinah's place, and it was arranged that I call to see the baby and bring Nipper home on my return.

The preacher caused a bit of trouble – I'd harnessed the horse and polished the trap ready for the end of the sermon, thinking he would start off then, but we had to wait until he'd had supper with one of the deacons before setting out.

Perhaps he had earned his supper. He'd given a fiery sermon full of the vigour of two hands and a powerful voice – I'd heard it coming through the walls of the chapel as I was cleaning the brass rail on the trap. His voice was searching out sinners, and I felt the sly darts of conscience as I polished the brass. Was it right to carry out the offices of pride on the Sabbath? Was it right to deck the chariot, even though it was for the High Priest? Yet, could we let the stranger priest, the visitor within our gates, go down with tarnished brasses? Would it not bring undying dishonour to the hospitality of the house? Better to risk offending against all the laws of the Sabbath than do this. Besides, retribution would, at least, be further removed. But wait! What was the punishment for the sin of pride, and pride aggravated; a sin in an undue season? Coals of fire and pits of brimstone! Hell's burning sands! But my hands had resolved the conflict whilst my head was still about it; the brasses were finished and the chariot was ready, and a quieter, less urgent note crept into the preacher's exhortations as if in sympathy, as if he had instantaneous knowledge that his gleaming carriage was at hand to take him down.

But there was still the supper. The deacon's house was not far away and I threw a rug across the horse's back and waited. After half an hour, the deacon's wife called down the street and I drove the trap to the door. The preacher came out with a shining red face, quietly subduing a belch with his handkerchief. He had a broad friar's face, wore spectacles, and a mop of white hair curled up under the brim of his broad hat. I helped him into the trap and tucked the rug around his legs. He gave a well-oiled smile to his hostess, raised his hat, and said in the same accents of evangelical fervour as he had used all the evening, 'Home, coachman!'

I clicked the horse into a quiet amble. The office of coachman to the High Priest didn't sit easily upon me, especially after waiting for so long at the gates of the Temple.

Yet we had not gone very far before we were the best of friends. He had done good service in that half-hour at the table and was full, among other things, of wise sayings. He said, 'You know, *bach*, you can't preach on a good meal. To preach fasting is my custom. The brain is clear and there are no rumblings and complainings in the belly. A man who goes into the pulpit after a full meal is two men: the lower

172

man, and the one above. The lower man finishes at his head, and would be sitting down and smoking his pipe and taking it easy; the other man would preach, but his preaching never leaves the ground but plods on like a sick man with a stitch in his side and gas in his belly. No, this is my text always, *bach*: preach fasting, and go home feasting.' He wiped his mouth comfortably with his red silk handkerchief, quietly singing a tripping hymn to the rattling wheels of the chariot, '*O Dduw y trugareddau mawr*' – 'O God of the large mercies.' He sang as though he was going home to another supper.

The road outside the village was full of couples walking out; of groups of boys who had just started work, sauntering slowly, calling out to the girls who passed in twos or threes, who were sedate until their ill-repressed giggles betrayed them. The preacher raised his hat to the couples, and lifted his hand benignly to the younger people. There were shouts and cat-callings from a crowd of boys, but the shining humour of his face never dulled. I had not the same ease of mind. The girls' glancing eyes were a challenge to me, sitting up remote and safe in the high seat of the trap. They seemed to say, 'Come down. Driving an old man is not a sport for a Sunday evening. We can tell you why the blood runs faster; why the day takes on a new strength in the evening. Come down and walk the mountain.'

I wanted to look back at the tall, slim girl with fair hair and a short upper lip, who glanced unsmiling at us as we passed, but the preacher chatted on, benevolently fixing me with his eye. He asked me how old I was; what I did at school; what I was going to do when I grew up. I answered abstractedly, unresponsively, too deep in the warm promise of the present to think of what would happen in three or four or even one year's time. Today is all. Now is the maying.

After a stiff climb, we reached the preacher's house. It was near the chapel, and both were built on a rocky headland that overlooked the Valleys like the preacher's rugged, nonconformist God. I dropped him at the gate. He was a kind old man, but I was relieved to have delivered him safely. I pressed Dick into a quick trot along the hard flint road to Brynllefrith. The air was full of the scent of honeysuckle from the close hedgerows.

I didn't stay long at Dinah's, only long enough to see the baby. It looked remote lying in the bottom of the cot. Nipper was quiet. I thought he was tired. Yet, after we left, I found there was something on his mind.

We were going gingerly down the steep hill before the straight stretch of road running down into the valley. Nipper was silent until his words burst out of him suddenly. 'I knew our Dinah would have a baby if she went to live there.'

'You knew what?' I asked, turning to look at him in surprise. His face was gloomy and disappointed. I had to smile, seeing Nipper where I had been myself – not so long ago, either.

'I knew she'd have a baby when she went to live in that street. They call it Incubator Avenue, and there are hundreds of kids and babies there, like nesting sparrows under the roof.'

I slackened the reins and gave the horse his head, laughing outright at Nipper's seriousness. His face was overcast. I knew how he felt – babies, and the suspicious manner of their coming, were a cloud swimming across the sky of his content. How did they come? Why did they come, when there was so much trouble in their coming? The mountain of clothes; the endless searching for a name – the correct name – and the risk of giving it the wrong name. Was it worth it? Would the howling piece of red flesh repay it all? Were not there already enough babies in the world? These were the questions which bothered Nipper. I could read his thoughts as a book. Yet I knew, also, that they would soon cease to worry him. Babies, as many other troubles, would soon be chased headlong out of the sky.

It was getting dark, and we stopped and took out the lamps from a box under the seat. They were big coach-lamps burning thick candles that were held in the long stem. As we were lighting them, two colliers who were returning from work crossed over from the other side of the road. They had recovered their pipes from the tree or the wall where they had hidden them whilst at work, and they were waiting for someone to come along with a match. They lit their pipes from one of the lamps and stood smoking, the acrid smell of their tobacco quickly spreading around them. As he closed the lamp one of them said, 'Wish I had a light like this in my place – I'd be able to see how high the top is.'

'Where you been?' asked the other, the white of his eyes showing up against his inky face, 'a wedding?'

'Somewhere grand, no doubt, with lamps like that.'

'No, just taking a preacher back.'

'A preacher, eh? He won't ride behind a better pair of lamps when he goes home.' They laughed quietly and, puffing at their pipes to make sure they had kindled them enough to last until they reached home, they passed on, singing 'Goodnight' out of the darkness.

Foreword by George Brinley Evans

George Brinley Evans was born in Banwen in 1925. He is a writer, sculptor and painter whose art has reflected a working life both in the mining industry of South Wales and as a soldier in World War II where he served with the 15th India Corps then the 12th Army in Burma. His short story collection *Boys of Gold* was published to critical acclaim in 2000 and was followed in 2006 by his evocative memoir *Where the Flying Fishes Play*. He still lives and works in Banwen.

Cover Image: The Hopkins Children – Aneurin, Hilda, Richard and Isaac at Blaenhonddan Uchaf, Mynydd March Hywel, Neath. Photographer unknown.

LIBRARY of WALES
FUNDED BY

Llywodraeth Cynulliad Cymru
Welsh Assembly Government

CYNGOR LLYFRAU CYMRU
WELSH BOOKS COUNCIL

LIBRARY OF WALES

So Long, Hector Bebb Ron Berry	£6.99 978-1902638805
Border Country Raymond Williams	£8.99 978-1902638812
Cwmardy & We Live Lewis Jones	£9.99 978-1902638836
Country Dance Margiad Evans	£6.99 978-1902638843
Ash on a Young Man's Sleeve Dannie Abse	£7.99 978-1905762255
The Dark Philosophers Gwyn Thomas	£7.99 978-1902638829
A Man's Estate Emyr Humphreys	£7.99 978-1902638867
In the Green Tree Alun Lewis	£7.99 978-1902638874
Rhapsody Dorothy Edwards	£7.99 978-1905762460
The Withered Root Rhys Davies	£7.99 978-1905762477
Sport Edited by Gareth Williams	£9.99 978-1902638898
Poetry 1900–2000 Edited by Meic Stephens	£12.99 978-1902638881
I Sent a Letter to My Love Bernice Rubens	£7.99 978-1905762521
Jampot Smith Jeremy Brooks	£7.99 978-1905762507
The Voices of the Children George Ewart Evans	£7.99 978-1905762514
Congratulate the Devil Howell Davies	£7.99 978-1905762514